Diamond's Pearl

By: D M Cummings

This book is a work of fiction. Names, characters, places and incidents are products of the author's imagination or are used fictitiously. Any resemblance to actual events or locales or persons, living or dead, is entirely coincidental.

The World Is Mine (TWIM) Publishing
P.O. Box 3086
Akron, OH 44309

~Revised 2023

ISBN: 978-0-9773854-1-6

Cover designed by Freeze
freezetheworld@gmail.com

Manufactured in the United States of America

INTRODUCTION

I don't know why I always felt like I had to have a man in my life, it didn't matter whose man it was, as long as he spent time with me and gave me something I didn't think that I could live without, "the dick." It may have a lot to do with me not knowing who my father was until I was grown with three kids of my own or maybe it was because I was deprived of my childhood, and I needed some closure. I have an older sister Regina, and a younger brother, Timothy who did basically anything that they wanted while I had to stay in the house cooking and cleaning. I felt like the black sheep of the family, no, more like Cinderella without the happy ending. I know I made a lot of bad decisions while growing up like sneaking boys into the house when I was twelve and thirteen, coming home late from school, lying to my mom saying that I was with my girls when, I was somewhere with a boy, in the back seat of a car, in the woods, the backyard, it didn't matter.

I *would usually hook up with the boys that no other girls wanted to talk to, you know, the buckteeth boy with the big glasses, and I would turn them out. I'd have them waiting for me outside the school like a lost puppy. No one knew that I was giving it to them, they just thought that I had all the boys wanting me and that's what I continued to let them think, and my boy-toys knew that they better not tell anyone, or they'd never get a taste of this good stuff again. When my friends and I would depart, I'd then hook up with them, most of the time I'd go to their house and watch pornos, to teach them something new. They loved me and I loved every bit of the attention. I just wish my mother would have talked to me instead of beating me or locking me in the attic for the bad choices that I made. I just wanted someone to love me.*

Dedication

This book is dedicated to the late Clifford Cummings Jr. I miss you big bro'. You have always inspired me to follow my dreams and to never give up. I will keep on pushing. I'll see you at the crossroads. Keep the memory alive. Always and forever.

January 29, 1972 - April 18, 2010

If God be for us, who can be against us.
Romans 8:31

ACKNOWLEDGEMENTS

First, I would like to thank God for giving me the strength to make it through life's challenging obstacles. Prayer changes things that no man can do. To my mom, dad and lil' bro' thanks for your support and encouraging words. To my three beautiful daughters', thanks for always cheering me up when I'm down, you all keep me strong. I would like to thank Freeze, for designing my book cover, you always do a wonderful job.

CHAPTER -1

Regina and Diamond are three years apart, but Regina wouldn't dare allow Diamond to hang out with her, and when she had a problem, Regina had no time to listen or give her advice like a big sister should. Regina worked two jobs, but when she wasn't at work she was either with her friends or on a date with some guy. Diamond usually sat outside her sister's bedroom door acting as if she was reading a book while she watched her get ready for a date. She usually put on a tight pair of jeans that showed her curvy shape or a short skirt that showed her big legs. Regina had what you call a "sha-dunk-a-dunk," a straight up ghetto booty. Diamond always wished she was just like her sister and able to do the things that she did. She had all the latest clothes, kept her hair and nails done and a ton of associates, unlike Diamond who only had a couple of females that she associated with. Diamond couldn't wait for Regina to leave so that she could go into her room and put on her make up and her fancy clothes.

"*Oh, I look nice, but not as nice as Regina*," Diamond thought. All Diamond wanted from Regina was a little of her time, but all they did was argue and fist fight.

Diamond ended up getting pregnant when she was fourteen, she hid it from her mother as long as she could, but her mother began to notice her not having a period after the third month of 'faking it'. Diamond had started to forget to wrap unused pads in toilet tissue and throw them in the trash, and with the temperature in Cottonwood, Arizona reaching one hundred and ten degrees most days, she couldn't wear big clothes to hide her once flat stomach.

"Come on Diamond, we're going on a road trip," her mother said. Diamond's mother, Rosetta, didn't play and she knew it, so she didn't ask any questions because she knew that it would only cause more drama. Rosetta took Diamond to the local women's clinic and made her take a pregnancy test and when the test came back positive, Diamond was every ho, bitch and slut there was under the sun and her life only got worse.

Diamond didn't have a clue who the father of her unborn child was. She did some calculations and narrowed it down to four people and when Nicole Marie, who she called Nikki, was born, she was beautiful with the prettiest big hazel eyes, but she was a little on the light side so Diamond assumed it was this guy named Mitch since he was the only light guy that she had encounters with in that time frame. Mitch was a good guy, but he was married. He and his wife were having problems at the time, and he was about to go to the military and Diamond didn't want to be a burden, so she told him to do what he could. Mitch was there, for the most part, because their daughter was beautiful, and he was about taking care of his responsibilities, but as time went on, he faded in and out of their lives. He had asked Diamond to get a paternity test, but she was afraid to find out the truth because Mitch was good to her, and their daughter and she didn't want that to end.

When Nikki turned one year old, her features changed drastically and so did her complexion and Diamond no longer thought that she was Mitch's baby, but she kept the thought to herself. Mitch was home from the military for a couple of weeks and he stopped by to see his daughter.
"Man Diamond, Nikki sure is getting a lot of color," Mitch said.
"I know, she's starting to look like me."
"Yeah, a little. Did you think about getting that paternity test because my wife and I are about to separate, and I want to get my kids so they will know each other. I was thinking of giving you ladies a break and keeping them for the summer."
"Well, you can count Nikki out because my mom is not

even trying to hear that, and plus, I'd miss her too much."
"I feel you, well look, Monday call and make an appointment so that we can get that done while I'm home."
"Monday I have a WIC appointment and that takes all day, so that's no good."
"Well, I'm home for two weeks, so see what you can do."
"Alright." He kissed Nikki and he left.
"What am I going to do, I can only stall this out for so long," Diamond thought.

Diamond called Mitch Monday evening.
"Hey, Mitch."
"Hey, what's up?"
"I called down to the paternity place and they don't have any openings until next month." She knew he had to return to base, and he wouldn't be back for at least another six months.
"Are you sure? I'm going to call down there in the morning to see if they could squeeze us in."
"I told them our situation, but they said they were sorry, but they were booked and if they have any openings they will call me."
"There's nothing they can do?"
"Nope." Diamond lied, she never called.
"Alright, I'll call you later." Mitch hung up the phone as Diamond wiped the sweat that had begun to bead on her forehead, and she laid down on the couch to try to get the flutters out of her stomach.

The next morning, Diamond called Stephon because he's the one that Nikki was beginning to look exactly like. She hated the thought because she hated him, and they didn't get along, not one little bit. She dialed the number and was just about to say forget it and hang up after the third ring, when he picked up the phone.

"Hello?," he said breathing heavily. Just the sound of his voice made her want to throw up.

"Were you busy?"

"Who is this?"

"Diamond." He smacked his lips.

"Oh, what's up?

"We need to talk. Can I come see you?"

"What, do we need to talk about?"

"Nicole."

"Who is Nicole?"

"Our daughter."

"That's your daughter and isn't Mitch playing daddy to her?"

"That's beside the point."

"Look, you need to get your shit together. I haven't seen you nor her in over a year so how in the hell do I know that baby is mine? The last time I saw her, she looked like a white man's kid. I have strong genes, look at my other two daughters, they look just like me."

"So does Nicole." There was a long silence. "Let's go and get a paternity test."

"Look, I'm chillin' with my girl right now and I don't have time for this shit," and then she heard a dial tone.

''I never should have called that bastard,'' she thought as she wiped the tears that were trickling down her cheek.

CHAPTER -2

Diamond had really gotten sick of her mother's rules, and her not allowing her to do anything and she wanted to move out, but her mother said that she had to graduate from high school first. She didn't have too many friends because her life was pretty boring, all she was allowed to do was, basically, sit on the porch. Her mother nor her sister would watch Nikki, and her mother wouldn't allow anyone else to either. She told her that since she wanted to be grown and make a baby, that she was going to take care of her baby.

Kendra was a good friend of Diamond's; she would come over and chill with her every now and then because she thought Rosetta's rules were ridiculous and she could just imagine what she must be going through. Kendra had a man, Greg, who occupied most of her time and although they had been together for quite some time, they were still lovebirds. Kendra had hooked Diamond up with a couple of guys that had tried to talk to her; that she had no interest in, and she went out with a couple of them, but her mom was so strict and made her be in by nine o'clock that it really didn't make any sense for her to go anywhere. Most of the time they stayed at her house, so Rosetta could monitor her visits, but she would sneak them into the bathroom that was right by the kitchen and give them some mad brain or a quickie, whichever they preferred, but after a couple of visits, they stopped coming to see her and every time she called them "they would call her right back," which they never did. She just didn't understand what she was doing wrong. "*Kendra has a boyfriend and they'd been together for almost a year, and they were having sex, I guess, and they can't seem to get enough of each other, maybe if I try to be like her, things will get better for me,*" *Diamond* thought.

Kendra had kind of gotten tired of Diamond trying to be 'all up in her business' all the time, asking about her sex life, wanting every detail on her dates and her phone conversations, so she tried to find her a man.

"Hey girl, what are you doing?"

"Nothing, just got done making us some peanut butter and jelly sandwiches."

"Can you talk for a minute?"

"Yeah, what's up?"

"One of Greg's friend's wants to meet you."

"Oh yeah?," she asked walking to another room so her mother couldn't hear her conversation. "What does he look like?"

"He's tall, brown-skinned, he's cool people. I think he'd be a good dude for you, he pretty much has his shit together. He doesn't have any kids and he's not a D-boy. He actually has a job. He still stays with his parents, but he's working on that."

"For real?," Diamond sounded so excited because she hadn't been with a man in over a month, and she needed someone just to hold her and talk to her on a regular basis.

"He's right here, do you want to talk to him?"

"What am I going to say?"

"Hold on, here he go."

"Kendra..." Diamond called, but she had already handed the phone to Greg's friend.

"Hello."

"Hi."

"Diamond, right?"

"Yeah, and your name is?"

"Earl."

"And how old are you?"

"Twenty-one, and you?"

"Seventeen."

"O.K., so when can I see you?"

"I don't know, could you put Kendra back on the phone and we can make some arrangements, because I don't have a car."

"She sounds pretty cool." Diamond heard Earl say while handing Kendra back the phone.

"So, Kendra, when do you have some free time? You know my mom will let me leave with you, as long as I take the baby."

"Next Saturday is good, so y'all can spend most of the day to get to know each other."

"Girl, I am so excited! He better be cute, and I hope he gotta big..."

"Look," Kendra interrupted, "I'll call you later," and she hung up the phone.

Saturday afternoon, Kendra went to pick up Diamond, who was wearing some denim daisy dukes, a white t-shirt and some white tennis shoes, she got into the car and could not stop smiling. When they arrived at Earl's house, Kendra introduced them again and they instantly clicked. Earl was very silly and loved to crack jokes, and he had Diamond's attention the whole afternoon. By six o'clock, Diamond was feeling Earl, but it was time to take her home. She had been so into their conversation, she hadn't realized how fast the time had gone by and she knew if she wasn't home when her mother said, she wouldn't be going anywhere else any time soon.

"Dang Kendra, I'm not ready to go. Can you call my mom and tell her we're going to be late?"

"No, you guys can exchange numbers and y'all can talk later. I have something to do tonight." Diamond finished up their conversation, got her baby's things together, who had been sitting in Earl's arms asleep for the past hour, and got up to leave. She gave Earl a hug and he walked them to the car, carrying the baby and putting her into her car seat. Diamond talked the whole way home telling Kendra everything that she had learned about Earl, which Kendra already knew, but she just listened and acted excited with her. Before Kendra dropped Diamond off, she had a few things to say to her because she knew how conniving Diamond was and she didn't want to see her homeboy go through any drama.

"I'm going to tell you this, Earl is my boy and he's a good dude, so you better do him right if you're trying to be with him like that."

"Girl, I feel a vibe, this is the one! You see how good he was with my daughter! I'm going to make sure I make him happy!"

"And it doesn't have to be with sex." Diamond just smiled as they pulled up in front of her house. Diamond got out of the car humming and smiling, Kendra just laughed. It was good to see her girl so happy, she deserved this happiness.

CHAPTER - 3

Several months went by and Diamond worried Kendra every weekend to make arrangements for her and Earl to see each other. After a while, her mother allowed him to come over their house because she wanted to meet him and see who had her daughter so in love, and she wanted to supervise their visits. Little did her mother know, Diamond was good, when she wanted sex, there was no stopping her. The first couple of times Earl came to visit and Diamond tried to have sex with him while her mother was upstairs, Earl wouldn't do it. She would hurdle on top of him, kissing him on his neck, his mouth and his chest to get him all aroused and he would just push her away.

"Man, this ain't cool, your mother is right upstairs. She'll hear us and she's not about to kill me."

"She's not going to come down here. Come on, I've been missing you since the last time we were together."

"I don't feel comfortable, knowing your mother is in the house." Diamond smiled as she began to unbuckle his pants. "That's what makes this so exciting." She pulled out his penis and began to give him oral sex. Earl tried to push her away, but it felt so good he just couldn't. He tried to hold in his moans, but he couldn't do that either, this was Diamond's specialty. She looked up at Earl so she could see his facial expressions, his eyes were closed, and his head was tilted back.

"Are you still going to tell me no?," she asked. Earl didn't answer, so she grabbed him by the hand and lead him toward the kitchen.

"You are crazy man, that's why I like you so much."

Diamond smiled, she was getting Earl right where she wanted him, in the palm of her hands where she could try to control him. Diamond opened the door to the basement, and they sat on the steps and were making passionate love. They were both moaning softly, and beads of sweat were on both of their faces. She was riding him like he had never been rode before until she heard someone coming from upstairs. She jumped up and ran into the kitchen where she began to pour herself a glass of juice. She knew how their house squeaked in certain spots when you had to pass to get downstairs and just about how much time it took to get from that spot. She quickly but quietly closed the basement door as her mother walked through the living room.

"Diamond?," her mother called in a questioning voice.

"Yeah," she answered innocently.

"Where are you?"

"In the kitchen. Why? Do you need something?"

"Yeah, you didn't hear your baby crying?"

"No, did she just start?," she asked as she walked out of the kitchen drinking her glass of red juice.

"No, she's been crying for a while." Diamond took her baby.

"Next time, I'm going to let her lay there and cry." She rolled her eyes as she kissed her baby on the forehead.

"What's the matter Boo-boo?" She asked her daughter as she sat down on the couch, hoping her mother would go back upstairs, but instead her mother sat on the couch beside her. Diamond knew she reeked of sex and prayed her mother wouldn't smell it.

"So," her mother began. Diamond's heart dropped and her mind started coming up with lies before her mother even asked the questions.

"Where's Earl?"

"*Easy one,*" she thought.

"He left."

"Why? What did you do?"

"I didn't do anything, he had something to do."

"So do you really like him?" Diamond was shocked because her mother never took any interest in the guys that she dated.

"Actually Mom, I do. No one has ever treated me like he does."
"I like him too; I think he'll be a great father for Nikki."
"I know, he's good with her and she loves him to death."
"Don't mess this up," her mother said as she got up to go back upstairs. Diamond waited a few minutes and then she put Nikki into her swing with a couple of toys and went back to the basement steps, but Earl was gone. She knew he had to be somewhere because they would have heard the door open. Diamond coughed and then cleared her throat and Earl came from under the steps.
"Man, I'm about to go. Rosetta is not about to shoot me." She took Earl back through the living room and out the front door. She sat on the porch with her daughter, and had Earl go through the neighbor's backyard so that her mother couldn't look out of her window and see him leaving. She knew her mother too well. Earl couldn't believe he had gone through with that. It was crazy and wild, but it was, actually exciting. He couldn't wait to see Diamond again. Since her mother interrupted her groove and she couldn't climax, Diamond went to her secret box that she kept hidden in the basement and retrieved her electric pink dolphin and put it to work, it didn't feel as good as Earl, but she made it work until she climaxed.

By the middle of the summer, you couldn't tell Diamond anything, she thought her stuff didn't stank. She kept her hair done, went and got a job at The Bank of Arizona, bought herself some decent clothes, and she had a good man. She was finally walking with her head up high. She had forgotten all about Mitch and hadn't given a second thought about Stephon. Everything was going great, and Diamond was the happiest she could remember being in her life, until one afternoon, she and Earl were into one of their freaky episodes and they were caught. Regina had called her mother because her car had broken down while she was on her lunch break, and it was about to get towed to the repair shop, so she needed a ride. Rosetta knew she wasn't going to want to come back out later to pick Regina up from work, and she didn't know what time Diamond was getting off, so she took Regina her car and Regina brought her back home, where she and Nikki took a nap.

Diamond didn't feel like catching the bus home that afternoon because it was humid and raining, so she called Earl to find her a ride. After fifteen minutes of waiting in the doorway off the bank, Earl and his cousin, James finally pulled up in the parking lot. Earl jumped out of the car.
"Baby, I'm so sorry. Traffic was so bad on the expressway, we tried..." Diamond cut him off.
"Don't worry about it baby, just make it up to me. You know how I like it." They both began to smile as he opened the car door for her so she could hurry up and get in. When they reached Diamond's house, they all went inside. Diamond saw that her mother's car wasn't in the driveway, and she became filled with excitement. She looked at Earl as she opened the door.
"Guess what?" Earl looked at her. "We are home alone." Earl looked at James who heard her comment.
"Let me make a phone call real quick." James called his female friend who didn't stay too far from Diamond. "Alright man, I'm about to go around Rena's for a minute. I'll be back in like an hour or so." Earl and James smacked hands and James went on his way. Diamond closed the door and she and Earl began to kiss passionately. Diamond took off her shirt and red bra and Earl began to suck her nipples as she unbuttoned his shorts and watched them fall to the floor. She could see his erection through his silk boxer shorts and that turned her on even more. She took off her red panties and pulled Earl towards her as she laid down on the couch. She pulled up her black skirt, just in case her mother returned home, then they

would be able to get dressed quickly. She knew her mother had to get Nikki out of the car, so it would take her a few minutes to get into the house. Earl kicked off his blue jean shorts, pulled his penis out of the hole in front of his boxers and put on a condom. He didn't want to be all the way naked either. He stuck his penis inside of her as she moaned with passion. They went at it for a good five minutes then Earl thought he heard something.

"Did you hear that?," he asked.

"What?"

"It sounded like somebody's upstairs."

"You're just paranoid, take off that condom and let me feel that good dick."

"I'm not ready for that yet. Are you sure nobody's here?"

"Positive." They continued and Diamond's mother walked downstairs. Diamond was so into it that she didn't hear the floor creek this time.

"Oh, hell naw! Let me go and grab my pistol! If I were you, I'd be gone by the time I get back!" Earl jumped up and put his shorts on as fast as he could, falling onto the couch, but still managing to get dressed.

"I told you I heard somebody." Diamond just sat there shaking her head in disbelief. She didn't know if she should stay there and suffer the consequences or if she should leave with Earl. He didn't wait for her to decide either, he rushed out of the door, went to the corner store, bought a pack of Black and Milds and a tall can of Colt 45. He walked around the corner to Rena's and sat on the curb and waited for James to come outside. When James saw his boy, he was shocked.

"What's up man? What happened?"

"Man, you're not going to believe this shit. Diamond's mother was in the house the whole time and she caught us."

"Oh, hell naw! She didn't try to kill your ass?"

"Man, I got up and got the hell out of there as fast as I could."

"Where's Diamond?"

"I don't know, I was worried about me. She said she was going to get her pistol. I know she won't shoot her own daughter, at least, I hope not, but I didn't know about me, so I got out of there."
"I don't blame you, but that's fucked up. So, what are you going to do?"
"I'm going to let things cool off and then I'll call her."
"If I were you, I would wait until she calls you."
"No, I'm a man, I'm going to have to face the music one day if we're going to be together."

Diamond never got up to get dressed, she just sat on the edge of the couch with her black skirt on, with her face buried in the palm of her hands crying. She knew her mother was going to kill her and there was no way out. She could have just left, but she didn't want to leave Nikki behind. Rosetta returned to the living room with her pistol in her hand. "That mutha fucka better be gone!" Diamond sighed heavily. "He left."
"I bet he did you nasty, triflin' bitch," and she grabbed Diamond off the couch by her arm. Diamond tried to snatch away, but her mother's grip was like vise grips.
"What the fuck is wrong with you, disrespecting my house like that? Do you think you gotta fuck everything that moves? You are nothing but a slut."
"You know what?" Diamond asked and her mother glared into her eyes trying to intimidate her. "I am nineteen years old and I'm tired of you talking to me like I don't have any feelings. You're not a saint. Regina, Tim and I don't have the same daddy and I've seen different men come and go around here. I know you were giving them some, or maybe that's why they don't come around anymore. You call yourself going to church every Sunday with your four-inch pumps and those little, short dresses on looking like a prostitute, dragging me and Nikki along like we're such a happy family, hoping to

meet a man. Well, God is not going to bless you acting like a whore. I'm sick of your strict rules and they only apply to me, because Regina comes and goes as she pleases. Tim does what he pleases, but I guess that's because he's a boy. Yeah, I've made some mistakes in the past, but I'm not perfect and all you do is put me down. I may be a black bitch to you, but I know who I am and if you got a problem with me, then I suggest you solve it on your own time, or maybe you should've had an abortion like you tried to make me do and then you wouldn't have to deal with me." Rosetta waited until she was done with her speech and then she smacked her across her face.

"Oh, you think you're grown now, huh? You done got you some and now you think your shit don't stank." Diamond grabbed the side of her face.

"I never thought I would say this, but fuck you, and as of this very second, you are no longer my mother. Fuck you and your rules, I'm leaving and I'm taking my daughter with me," Diamond said as tears stormed down her face. Rosetta grabbed her by her hair and dragged her to the floor.

"Fuck me? I brought you into this world and I'll take you out if you ever disrespect me like that again, and Nikki's not going anywhere because you don't have anywhere to go. You don't have any friends and Earl still stays with his mama so that leaves you stuck right here with me."

"Please, I'll sleep in a box under a bridge before I sleep here again."

"You go and sleep in your box, but you leave Nikki here."

Diamond packed up all she could carry and walked to the pay phone and called Kendra and told her everything that had happened. Kendra came and picked her up.

"Look Diamond, you can stay here for tonight and that's it. This is not just my place, and I don't want Greg to feel uncomfortable in his own home." In reality, Kendra knew how Diamond was, she would try her best to fuck up your relationship just because she could. She trusted Greg, but he was a man and although all men aren't dogs, some women are, and Kendra wasn't even going to put Greg in that predicament. Diamond called Earl, who hadn't made it home yet, so she spoke to his mother.

"Hello, mama Rita, this is Diamond. If it's alright with Earl, can I stay with you until I find somewhere else to stay?," and she started to cry. "My mom put me out today."

"Why? What happened?"

"Well, Earl and I...," and she began to chuckle, "and well my mom... you know."

"What? She caught y'all?

"Yeah and she basically put me out. She wouldn't allow me to bring my daughter because I basically don't have anywhere to stay."

"Girl, I don't care what Earl says, you go and get your baby and y'all can stay with me as long as you need to." Diamond did just that.

CHAPTER - 4

Winter was beginning and Mama Rita was ready for Diamond and her spoiled baby to go, but she couldn't just put them out on the streets. Since Diamond nor Earl had a car, she was taking Diamond back and forth to work every day, which was on the other side of town. She was taking the baby to her appointments, Diamond to hers and it was becoming a task. She made Diamond catch the bus a few times, but she still had to keep Nikki while Diamond was working. Mama Rita started making Diamond give her one hundred dollars a month to help with food and utilities, which Diamond didn't mind, although she was trying to save up for a car, but she continued to run into obstacles, so she decided to do it the dirty way. She began by taking small amounts of money out of everyone's account that came to her window at the bank, but that wasn't adding up fast enough, so she had Earl and his cousin James come through the drive-thru a couple of times. She would remember account numbers and give them a withdrawal slip and take money out of older people's accounts that didn't bank frequently within the month, and then she started taking larger amounts out of people's accounts that held over ten thousand dollars. Her drawer had come up short a few times and the bank manager, Carmen Wright, finally pulled her into her office and asked her about the money. She claimed she didn't know what happened so Carmen wrote her up and told her that the next time, she would be terminated since neither time it was a very large amount that was missing. Diamond became scared and decided to do the right thing, but by then people had begun to call in to complain about their accounts. Carmen reviewed all of the tapes, but didn't see anything that looked suspicious, so she went a step farther and began to check the times the money was withdrawn from the complaining customer's accounts, and everything pointed to Diamond. Carmen called the police, as well as Rosetta, to inform her that Diamond was on her way to jail because Carmen knew Rosetta from high school, and she had given her the job. Carmen then called Diamond into her office, again.

“Alright, Ms. Diamond, is there anything you would like to tell me?” She looked at her boss and then the police officer and nonchalantly replied.

“Nope,” while shaking her head. “Is there something you would like to know?,” she asked.

“Well, since you want to get smart, we have been getting a lot of complaints about people’s accounts being short and everything points to you.”

“I don’t know what you’re talking about.”

“Well, after adding everything up, we’ve estimated that you’ve taken over ten thousand dollars from various accounts. Now, you can return the money, or we will have to arrest you for embezzlement.

“I don’t have your money.” And that wasn’t a lie. Diamond and Earl had been living the good life and they spent every dime of that money. They were eating out almost every night. They bought themselves a 1999 tan Chevy Malibu for three thousand dollars. They bought new shoes, clothes, the baby new clothes, and new furniture for the apartment they were planning on getting. A couple of weeks prior, Diamond had signed up for housing assistance and was now on the waiting list. Diamond ended up getting arrested, Mama Rita put her out, Rosetta gained temporary custody of Nikki and she and Earl broke up. Diamond spent forty-five days in jail, where she tried to kill herself because, in her opinion, her life was over. She was later diagnosed with being bipolar and was put on probation for three years. Diamond was very angry that she was caught before she could quit because now she was back to square one, living back with her mother, and once again, she had total control of her life. In the back of Diamond’s mind, she knew she couldn't stay with her mother because she had gotten so used to her freedom and now that she was single, she planned on doing her own thing and enjoying her life as she pleased.

Three days had passed, and Diamond knew she had to go, but she had to figure out where. She knew Kendra wasn't having it, so she went to her cousin, Mario. He didn't stay very far from Rosetta, but it was far enough. Mario was seven years older than Diamond and he had it going on. He was like the big brother she never had, and she looked up to him. At twenty-six, he owned a three-bedroom house, two nice cars and always had a pocket full of money. Mario was a real businessman, he owned a franchise of barbershops in several cities throughout Arizona, he owned an arcade room and he worked with unfortunate children. Mario always felt sorry for Diamond but didn't know what to do. His Auntie Rosetta was strict and stuck to her rules. Diamond was almost twenty now and she had graduated from high school. Mario took her in, and Rosetta let her go, but she kept Nikki and Diamond didn't care because she didn't want to be tied down anyway. The day Diamond was free, she went buck wild. She started sleeping with everything that looked like a stick; Mario's friends, his cousins on his dad's side, because she didn't think that were family, because they weren't 'blood related'. Mario saw what she was doing and tried talking to her, but it went in one ear and out of the other because she finally felt loved. Guys were blowing up her cell phone and knocking down Mario's door to get to her, because she did what she had to do to make sure they came back for more.

A month had passed, and Diamond received her letter from the Housing Department, and they placed her in the projects where she had access to everybody's man. Big mistake, major! Mario was relieved because he was ready for her to leave a long time ago, but he didn't want to put her out on the street. He tried taking her out and spending time with her but that just allowed her to meet other men and that was not what he wanted. He was trying to show her that just because a man takes you out and spends time and money on you doesn't mean that you have to sleep with them, make them work for it and he will respect you so much more. Mario would tell her that all the time, but Diamond's main concern was not respect, it was satisfaction.

CHAPTER - 5

Mario decided to take Diamond out to celebrate her getting her first place. They entered "The Buzz", one of the hottest clubs in Arizona, and it was jumping. It was packed from wall to wall. Diamond knew it was around the first of the month and everyone comes out then, so she put on her "fuck'em outfit," which was a very short, tight, white mini skirt, a pair of high heel sandals with straps that wrapped around her legs, almost up to her knee, and a pink halter that left her back and arms out. Ever since Diamond gave birth to Nikki, she had picked up weight and had a nice little shape. She did her hair real nice, with a bunch of micro-curls and put on her white stunner shades. For the first time in a long time, Diamond felt beautiful. They entered the club, and all eyes were on her. The guy collecting the money looked her up and down.

"Damn shorty, do I need to pat you down for weapons because you are killin'em?" Diamond smiled, put a little twist in her hips and kept walking. They made their way to the bar where Mario ordered them both a shot of Patron and a Corona. Mario drunk his drinks and then excused himself to talk to some people who he saw sitting across the bar.

"I'll be right back, lil' cuz. Are you alright?"

"Yeah, I'm fine." Diamond sat at the bar finishing up her drink and rocking to the music. The DJ was hot, he kept everyone on the dance floor all night. Diamond was just about to take a sip of her beer when she spotted a guy across the bar standing up against the wall bobbing his head to the music.

"Damn he is fine. I've got to get to know him," Diamond thought. She finished her beer and took her shot of Patron to the head, got up from her seat and headed in his direction. She didn't have a clue as to what she was going to say, but she was going to make it good. She stood beside him as she bobbed her

head to the music as she smiled. The guy looked in her direction and the games began. She put her glasses on the edge of her nose and gave the guy a distraught look.
"Excuse me, do I know you from somewhere?" He looked at her slowly shaking his head no.
"Did I fuck you?" He began to choke on the Bud Ice he was drinking. Diamond shrugged her shoulders and started laughing. The guy had never been approached like that by any female.
"You are crazy," said the young man.
"No," she said extending her hand. "Diamond" and the conversation sparked from there. They danced to a couple of songs; he bought her a couple of drinks and they exchanged numbers. That weekend he helped her move and a week later, William moved in with her.

Diamond and William's relationship was going well, but he just couldn't put it down sexually like she wanted him to, so when he left to go to work, so did she. William worked from three to eleven as a security guard at a boarding school, and that worked fine for her because she usually didn't get up until around two in the afternoon.

One afternoon, Diamond was sitting on her stoop when she spotted another victim. She was already dressed in an Apple Bottom jumper that fit like a glove, she had added some tracks to the back of her hair to give it some length and to give herself a different look. She would get up every day and fix herself up nice so she could walk to the store or just sit outside. As she was sitting outside, she saw this guy riding his bike through the parking lot. He stopped to talk to a couple of guys who were two complexes over. She sized him up, blue and white Jordan's, Coogi blue jean shorts, and his Coogi shirt and hat were matching. Diamond stood at the edge of the grass and just stared in their direction until they looked up, and she motioned her finger for the one to come to her. They all began to point to themselves, and she shook her head no until they got to the one she was referring to. They all began to laugh and slap hands. The guy with the Jordan's on rode his bike over to where she was standing, and he was even finer up close. He was tall dark and handsome. He removed his hat to wipe the sweat off his forehead and his hair was neatly braided to the back. When he smiled his teeth were perfect and pearly white. He had on a scent of cologne that she had never smelled before, but it smelt so good it made her eyes close every time she got a whiff of it. He introduced himself as Tyron. He and Diamond talked for a while, then he left her with his cell phone number, and she invited him back later that night.

Diamond thought she was slick, she would have guys over while William was at work, but she always made them leave by 10:30, enough time for her to clean up, get a shower and burn a musk incense to kill any weird smells. William knew what was going on, but he felt their relationship came about too fast and as long as he had a roof over his head, a meal to eat, some free pussy and his own money, he didn't care what she did. Until she became pregnant, and then everything changed. He didn't want her going anywhere, he didn't want guys calling her, he wanted her all to himself. Everyone in the hood continued to tell him that she was a ho and always would be and that he couldn't change her, but he didn't listen.

He decided to take a couple of days from work without letting Diamond know. He got ready for work like he did every day, but instead of going to work, he went over to his boy, Bruce's house and they traded cars. Bruce had a big van with tinted windows and he and Diamond had never met. William parked the van across the parking lot, backed in so he would be facing Diamond's door and reclined the seat. He wasn't there a good half an hour when he saw Tyron walking through the yards. He didn't even knock on Diamond's ajar door, he just walked in. He saw the front door close, and his heart was broken. William waited a half an hour, which seemed like six hours to him, for Tyron to get out of their house, but he hadn't come out yet. He wasn't going to go crazy over a girl he barely knew, even though she was carrying his child, so he thought. He sat there for another fifteen minutes, then he decided to get out of the car. He used his key to open the door and quietly closed it back. He heard the moaning from the bottom of the steps. He didn't want to walk in on them, because that visual would have stayed in his head forever and he wanted some action. It was a hot summer day in the projects, so everyone was outside. William turned the heat up as high as it would go, he turned the oven to broil and sat down to watch the television that was already on. He waited a good five minutes, enough time for the house to get nice and hot, then he took his lighter and held it up to the smoke detector in the kitchen. When it started to beep, he did the same to the one closest to the stairs and waited. Fifteen seconds later, Diamond and Tyron came running down the stairs, half dressed. Tyron ran outside and when Diamond saw William standing there smiling, she stopped in her tracks.

"What the hell are you doing here?," Diamond asked.

"I thought I lived here, and you're blaming me for that bastard ass child you're carrying. Hmmm, I don't think so. That brotha came in here like it was a routine. I'm about to get my shit because I'm out."

"I don't care, if you would have been putting it down like Tyron, I wouldn't've had to cheat. You're always so tired when you get off work. You get your shit off and then you leave me wet and wanting more. So, I went for mine."

"You are one nasty bitch! If I wasn't a man, I would slap the shit out of you, but you might like that, so instead, I'm going to get my shit and bounce."

"Leave! But you <u>are</u> going to take care of my baby."

"Bitch please. I need to see a paternity test first."
"Yeah, child support will be contacting you in eight months."
"That's cool, as long as you don't call me." William gathered all his things and packed them into Bruce's van and went on his way, and that was the last he'd seen of Diamond.

Eight months later, Diamond gave birth to a seven pounds, two ounces and 21 inches long little boy who she named Brandon Christopher. She tried to contact William on several occasions. He came to the hospital and saw the baby and knew it wasn't his, so he never returned any of her calls. She went to child support, and they ordered a paternity test. He took it with no hesitation to get the truth as soon as possible so she would stop calling him. As William thought from day one, the results were negative and Diamond didn't look any further for her son's father because as far as she was concerned, she was the father.

CHAPTER -6

Diamond began to notice a lot of guys trying to get with her, for all the wrong reasons, of course, but she didn't care, she was still happy. She was getting the attention she had been striving for all her life. She had someone to talk to, hold her and to be inside of her, even if it was only for a short time. She felt wanted and loved. Diamond wanted that feeling so often that she was sleeping with three to four different guys a week, sometimes more than that in one day. Everything was wonderful, and Diamond hadn't been this happy since she and Earl were together. She had a beautiful week with a couple of her boy-toys, she had even met a few more. Some of them had begun to buy her gifts, because they actually liked her. She was so busy into her own world that she didn't know the difference between lust, love, and sex; it was all the same to her.

One morning, Diamond woke up and called a couple of people to set up her day. She ran herself a hot bubble bath to try to make her feel better from all the drinking and smoking of marijuana the night before. She went into the bathroom to relieve herself of the urine she had held all night because she was too tired to get up. She sat down on the toilet and her vagina felt swollen, she thought maybe it was from all the rough sex that she had the night before. She leaned back against the toilet, let her legs fall open, rubbed her vagina lips along with the swollen area around her hole, and inserted her finger inside herself. It burned!
"Ouch! What the fuck is that shit?," she said aloud. She looked under the sink and took out the mirror she used to do her hair with and put it between her legs so she could get a view of her vagina. That's when she noticed what appeared to

be a blister. She rubbed her fingers across the blister and became puzzled.

"*Maybe he scratched me when he was fingering me. It'll go away in a couple of days," she* thought. She got into the bathtub and soaked for an hour before she got dressed. She held off from sex for the next couple of days, which was extremely hard. She began to masturbate at night and in the morning, she'd lay in the bathtub and let the warm water run on her vagina while she rubbed it until she climaxed. By the middle of the week, her blister turned into blisters, and they began to pus. That made her finally call Dr. Reed's office to make an appointment. When she told the nurse, April, her symptoms, she wanted her to be seen the next day.

The next morning, Diamond was trying to hold back her tears as she waited for the bus because Earl had kept the Malibu since it was in his name. Diamond didn't have any use for it while in jail. She arrived at Dr. Reed's office and was seen right away. They gave her a sheet and told her to take off everything below the waist and unfasten her bra. She did as she was told and when Dr. Reed came in to examine her, she began to cry.

"What's the matter?," Dr. Reed asked.

"I just want this to be over with."

"I'll get this over as quickly as possible." He asked her about her last period and all ``the procedure questions then told her to lay back, put her feet into the stirrups and to scoot to the end of the table. He examined her and then told her the bad news. Diamond had herpes. He explained to her that there was no cure, and she broke down crying again and was unable to stop. He offered her counseling, but she refused.

"Look Diamond, there is medication that will control it, but it won't cure it. I need you to give me a list of names of everyone you've been sexually active with in the last thirty days." She looked at him out of the corner of her eye and

began to cry even harder. He rubbed her back to try to calm her down as she sat in a chair with her head laying on her arms on the table. After about ten minutes, the crying suppressed.
"Can I just write the names down myself?"
"Sure." He handed her a 2"x3" piece of tablet paper. She shook her head from side to side.
"May I please have a bigger sheet?" The doctor gave her a distraught look as he went into a drawer and retrieved a full sheet of paper.
"Is there any way you can tell me around the time I got this?"
"Probably within the last week or two. It's kind of hard to say." Diamond thought as hard as she could as she wrote down the names. She came up with fourteen names and she narrowed it down to who could have given her the disease. It was only three new guys that she had been with and two of them had worn a condom. The other guys were guys she'd messed with in the past that she hung out with on a regular basis. Most of them used condoms too, because they had girlfriends, but Diamond would do things that their girlfriends wouldn't do. She was the type that would do something 'strange' for a little bit of change. She handed Dr. Reed the list of guys she'd been with in the past two weeks, and he looked at it.
"Oh, I just needed the names of the guys in the last thirty days." Her eyes filled with tears as she put her head down to look at the floor. She was too embarrassed to be honest and tell him that it had been close to twenty guys that she had been with in the past thirty days. He picked up the list feeling like maybe he should have kept his mouth shut.
"Look Diamond, I'm not here to judge you, but this is important. We need to notify these guys so that they can be tested. I need their phone numbers too, so that I can contact them."
"I don't know all of their numbers," and she looked up at him. "Will Facebook accounts do?" Diamond wrote down the

numbers that she knew, and Dr. Reed gave her a few sample packages of medication along with her prescription. He explained to her that the disease could usually only be spread when it's active, that she should still practice safe sex all the time and that the safest sex is abstinence. She cried all the way back home and didn't care who saw her. She was trying to think of some type of revenge to get the guy back for ruining her life. When she got home, she called her cousin, Big Tone, who was a straight- up thug and was down for whatever. He called her back within the hour because she had told him on his voicemail that it was an emergency.

"What's up, lil' cuz?," and she started crying.

"I'm on my way over." He arrived at her apartment five minutes later, she was sitting on the couch with her eyes blood shot red from her crying. "What happened?"

"I met this guy last week and we had sex and now I got herpes." She began to cry harder.

"What, you didn't make him use a condom?"

"It all happened so fast. We had been drinking and smoking and he took advantage of me. I think he might have put something in my drink." She looked at him out of the corner of her eye. Big Tone knew Diamond, oh-too-well and always knew when she was lying.

"Oh, yeah?"

"Yup."

"So, what do you want me to do about it?"

"I want you to beat his ass."

"What's his name?"

"Kevin."

"Short Kevin that stay in the hood?"

"Yeah," she answered looking a bit embarrassed.

"I know that cat. I'll go holla at him."

"I'm coming too." Diamond and Big Tone got into his black Lexus with the twenty-inch rims and headed to Kevin's house.

"Stay in the car. I'll be right back." Big Tone got out of the car, walked up Kevin's driveway and knocked on the door. He came to the door wearing a pair of blue jeans and no shirt.
"What's up dude? I need to politic with you," Big Tone said. Kevin came outside onto the porch.
"What's up?"
"What's up with you and my cousin, Diamond?" Kevin smacked his lips.
"Nothing."
"Well, she said that you put something in her drink so that you could fuck her and then you burnt her."
"Man, no disrespect, but your cousin a ho. I met her at the bar about a week or two ago and we had a few drinks then went to breakfast. She stayed the night at my house and the next morning, we took a shower together. She left and told me to make sure I called her, but I haven't gotten around to it yet."
"Alright, I wanted to hear your side of the story. Now, I'm going to bring y'all together." Tone signaled for Diamond to get out of the car. She walked up the driveway and got between Big Tone and Kevin.
"Now you said he put something in your drink?" She ignored Tone's question and got in Kevin's face.
"You ruined my life you bastard," Diamond taunted. Kevin put his hands in the air.
"You can't be mad at me. I told you no, I didn't want to do nothing, and you started sucking my shit. I tried to push you away, but you were persistent... and that shit felt good. I'm not going to tell you no but so many times."
"You could have told me you had herpes."
"You ain't my woman. I don't have to tell you shit."
"That's fucked up," she said as tears streamed down her face.
"Big Tone, whip his ass. He don't even have any remorse for this shit."

"Ah man, my hands are tied on this one lil' cuz. You put yourself in this situation. You should have made him strap up if you wanted to fuck him that bad."

"Tone, that's fucked up! You're supposed to have my back!"

"If he would have raped you, then that would have been different, but that shit was consensual." Tone started walking back to his Lexus. "I'll be in the car when you're ready." Any other time, Tone wouldn't have asked any questions, he would have just started swinging, but Diamond had gotten him into so much mess in the past by lying, that he started asking questions before he reacted. She came to the car a few minutes later, crying her eyes out.

"There's no need to be mad about it. You just gotta take care of yourself and be more careful."

"That's easy for you to say." Tone dropped Diamond off at her house and went on about his day. The next week, Diamond had somebody else's man lying between her sheets.

CHAPTER - 7

Diamond's sex addiction had gotten worse, she never told anyone about her "problem," but would masturbate when she felt she was going to have an outbreak. She now had four partners a week and didn't care if they put on a rubber or not. If they did that was cool, but if they didn't, oops! Their fault. This went on for the next couple of months, until she missed her period. She went to the pharmacy and bought a pregnancy test, and it was positive. Of course, with all the partners she had so close together, she didn't know whose it was, so she blamed it on the guy who she'd been with the most and knew he'd take responsibility. Diamond called Tyron that evening to share what she thought was good news.

"Tyron, baby I got some good news."

"What's up?"

"I'm pregnant." The line went silent.

"Hello?," then she heard a dial tone. Five minutes later, Tyron was knocking at the door.

"What did you say?" The look on his face showed her that he was not happy.

"How do you know it's mine? Man, you've been around a couple of corners lately."

"Well, I did my calculations, and it points to you."

"Man, you know my girl just had a baby and we live together. Don't try to fuck up our shit."

"You fucked up y'all shit by fucking me. Now, you're going to take care of your responsibilities, or you will be sorry." Tyron turned around and walked out the door. "Oh, and it would be wise to tell your girl because I know you'll hate for her to hear it on the street," and she slammed the door as she giggled.

The next couple of months, Diamond had Tyron eating out of the palm of her hands so she wouldn't let the word out. He wasn't trying to lose his family, but Diamond was a good lay and she made sure her men were satisfied, no matter what she had to do. She'd call him in the middle of the night for food, early in the morning for money or a quickie and since they stayed in the same projects, only three buildings over, it was easy for him to run over there and be back before he was missed by his girl, Keysha. After a couple months of the same routine, Keysha became suspicious.

"Where do you keep running to in the middle of the night?"

"I'm trying to handle some business."

"*Typical response*," she thought.

"Yeah, OK." From that day forward, every time he left, she would be in the window or on the porch watching where he was going. He went the same way every time, through the neighbor's backyard. Now, she knew it was another girl and she was going to find out who she was. That night when Tyron went to bed, she turned his phone on vibrate after she went through his phone log, of course, and waited for this mystery lady to call. Diamond called every night like clockwork and this night was no exception. At 1:18 AM, Tyron's phone rang.

"Hello?" Keysha answered and Diamond hung up. She hadn't blocked out her number like most females would have done because she didn't care if his girl knew she called. Keysha got up and went into the bathroom and called her back.

"Who is this?"

"Who is this?," Diamond asked in a sassy tone.

"This is Tyron's woman, Keysha, now who is this calling my man?"

"This is Diamond."

"Well, what do you want? It's one o'clock in the morning."

"I wanted him to come see me."

"Well, he's asleep and if he wasn't, he wouldn't be to see you."
"I can't tell. He comes here every night and brings me something to eat."
"I doubt that one. He don't care about you enough to get out of his bed and leave his family to come see no scalawag."
"He probably don't care about me like that, but I bet you he cares about this baby that I'll be having in five months."
"Bitch, don't get fucked up." Diamond laughed as she hung up the phone. Keysha went back into the bedroom and turned on the light, threw the phone and it hit Tyron in the back of his head.
"Get your ass up! Who the fuck is Diamond and why is she talking about she's pregnant by you?" Tyron sat up rubbing his head.
"Why the fuck are you trippin'?"
"You gon' be trippin' if you don't answer my questions."
"Would you please come back to bed?" She knocked everything off the dresser and onto the floor.
"Get up! We're about to go and see her."
"I'm not going anywhere."
"Well, I bet you won't sleep tonight. If that phone would've rang, I bet your ass would have gotten up." They continued to argue until the sun came up. The next couple of times Diamond called, Tyron ignored her calls. She'd hang up and call right back, but he wouldn't answer.

Three days later, Diamond knocked at Tyron's door. Luckily his girlfriend wasn't at home. He came to the door.
"What the fuck are you doing here?" He was furious.
"You didn't answer my calls, so I wanted to make sure everything was alright."
"It's fine. Now get the fuck away from here."
"Only if you promise to come see me later."
"I promise." Diamond headed home just as Keysha was

pulling back up in the parking lot. She had asked around about who Diamond was and had a pretty good description of her. She knew that bitch was leaving her house and she was going to find out what she wanted. Keysha knew which parking lot Diamond stayed in but wasn't sure as to which apartment. She got back into her car and drove around to Diamond's parking lot and parked on the street where she could see every apartment. She sat there for about two minutes and waited for Diamond to go into her apartment. "*Yeah,*" she thought. She went back home to drop off her kids, parked her car and decided to go pay Diamond a little visit. She walked through the yards, just as Tyron did every night and knocked on the door that she saw her go into. Diamond knew what Tyron's girl looked like because she had seen her and Tyron out on several occasions.

"May I help you?," Diamond asked, being sarcastic.

"Yeah, are you Diamond?"

"In the flesh." She said as she waved her hands over her body.

"So, you're the bitch that's supposed to be pregnant by my man, Tyron?"

"Yup." Diamond said smiling while rubbing her stomach. It was like Diamond was trying to rub it in her face. Keysha was upset and hurt because she was good to Tyron, she did everything for him and he played her like this. She turned around to walk away.

"*Either I'm going to kill this bitch or I'm going to just have to let him go.*" She thought as tears began to form in her eyes.

"Hey," Diamond called out to her. "Don't be mad, we can all be cool because he's going to take care of his son." That broke Keysha's heart because she and Tyron had been trying for a boy, but they ended up with two girls.

"Fuck you."

"No, that's Tyron's job." Keysha turned around and charged Diamond with full force and tackled her to the ground.

"Bitch, you're not about to fuck up my relationship!" She yelled while punching her in the face. "I put too much into this relationship and I'm not about to lose out to some stankin' ho." She got up, kicked Diamond in the stomach and Diamond grabbed her foot. Keysha knelt on the leg that Diamond was holding and began to punch her in the stomach and anywhere else she could. She stood back up and Diamond was lying on the ground holding her stomach. Keysha took off running back home to her man and cried on his shoulder.

"I love you baby and we need you in our lives. Don't ever let a bitch come between us." She took Tyron's phone off his hip and kept it for the next couple of weeks. She ignored all of Diamond's calls and made sure her man did not leave her sight.

Diamond lost her baby and was now looking for revenge on Tyron's girlfriend, Keysha.

CHAPTER - 8

Diamond was lonely now. Ever since the incident with Keysha, she was considered "hot", and no one wanted to be bothered with her and risk messing up their relationship or their reputation. Diamond wanted to be a part of Nikki's life so she could get closer to Earl. Earl had rekindled his relationship with Rosetta and was helping her take care of Nikki. Although he wasn't her father, he loved her like he was and felt she deserved a better life. Diamond was too much into herself to give her that. She walked to Rosetta's house daily to get Nikki. She took her to the park, and bought her clothes and toys, trying to make up for lost time and to show Earl and her mother that she wanted to be a part of her life. Earl and Diamond started spending a lot of time together with Nikki by taking her to parades, amusement parks, and everywhere else as a family. Earl started staying at Diamond's house daily, not necessarily living there, but sleeping there most nights. Diamond was happy with that because she had the only man that she thought ever really loved her back in her life. She was treating Earl like a king: having his dinner ready when he came home from work, giving him sponge baths and of course, sex every night, any way he wanted it. They were so in love that Rosetta even allowed her to keep Nikki a couple of nights a week and that was fine because Earl was home to help her.

One morning, Earl went to work at his normal shift of 6:30 AM to 3:30 PM at the Medical Center as a housekeeper and was given a promotion to nursing assistant in the Intensive Care unit and his shift changed to 11 PM to 7 AM. This gave him a five dollar an hour increase in his wages, and they could definitely use the money. Earl wanted more than the project life. He wanted a home for Nikki and Diamond and one day, a child of his own and this was their break. Diamond was so excited. Every day she would look for a house, but they just couldn't agree upon anything. Diamond was searching in the hood and Earl was looking in a more sophisticated area.

A few weeks passed and Diamond became tired of being home alone at night; she missed Earl holding her and rolling over and just knowing that someone was there. Although Earl did hold her at night before he went to work, he would usually lay down around eight at night, and made love to her, if he wasn't too tired. After a while, that once or twice a night became once or twice a week and Diamond became bored with her little pink vibrator because she wanted that body heat and a back to stroke. Diamond and Tyron had become friends again and on the rare occasion that they did have sex, he wore a condom. Diamond really wanted to be more with him because he was a great lover, but she didn't want to have to deal with Keysha's crazy butt, again, so she dealt with it. She considered Tyron a friend, also, and enjoyed playing spades or Phase 21 and drinking with him and his friends until two or three in the morning. This had become an everyday thing and Diamond was loving it.

One night, Earl got up and went to work, even though, he felt sick, he went anyway because he needed the money. He figured he would get better as time passed. Earl worked three hours and continued to throw up and have diarrhea, so he went home. He got out of his car and heard the music blaring out of the apartment before he even reached their stoop. He shook his head with disgust and was about to turn around and go to his mother's house so he could get some rest, but something told him to go inside. Earl entered the apartment where he saw four guys sitting at the dining room table playing cards, smoking blunts and drinking beer. There was a gallon of Grey Goose vodka sitting in the middle of the table and a half gallon of orange juice and cranberry juice on the sink. The music was so loud, and they were so into their game, that no one saw or heard Earl walk in. There was some guy lying on the couch asleep and Diamond had her feet between Tyron's legs massaging his "stuff."

"*She's not ever going to change,*" Earl thought. He went upstairs to check on Nikki, who was sitting up in her bed talking to some guy Earl had never seen before. "Dude, what are you doing in my daughter's room?" The guy jumped up off the end of the bed.

"Man, this ain't your daughter, we sit up here and talk every night."

"*Was this some sort of pervert? It's two o'clock in the morning, why is Diamond letting this grown, drunk ass man spend time with the child I've been taking care of,*" Earl thought. He was furious. He picked up Nikki and took her downstairs. He turned the music down and everyone turned and looked at him.

"It's time for y'all to go." The guy that was upstairs ran downstairs.

"Who the fuck is this chump, trying to come up in here regulating and trying to check somebody? This ain't your crib! This our hang out spot! This what we do every night!" Earl looked at Diamond and she just shook her head because she knew that she had fucked up.

"We not leaving until Diamond say it's time for us to go," said the guy that was upstairs.

"Man, you're making a simple situation bad for no reason," Earl said.

"Fuck you, dude." Earl wanted them to leave because he had a few things to say to Diamond about having that man up in Nikki's room like that and they weren't leaving fast enough, and it was pissing him off.

"Diamond, tell your little friends that they have to go."

"Man, y'all go ahead and go. I'll catch up with y'all later," Diamond said. They all got up and gathered their things and left. One of the guys bumped Earl on purpose.

"Mark ass punk," he said as he passed him. Earl shook his head in disgust. When everyone was gone, the argument began.

"What the fuck is wrong with you? Are you that fucked up in the head that you just let grown ass men chill up in your daughter's room at two o'clock in the morning? My mother always warned me about messing with you little petite girls. I don't think your brains are developed all the way."

"What are you talking about? That's her uncle."

"That's not your brother or your mother's brother and she don't know her real daddy, so I know it's not his brother and even if it was he still didn't have any reason to be in her room like that. She had on her pajamas and the music was too loud for you to hear what was going on. You don't know what that pervert was doing to my baby! I see why your mother don't let you keep her. You are a stupid..." Earl paused, he never called a woman a bitch, but he almost did this time.

"A stupid what?," Diamond asked.

"I don't have time for this shit. Me and my daughter are going to my mother's house," Earl said. "You are not taking my daughter anywhere. This ain't your child."

"Oh, that's how you want to play? Fuck you and don't call me for nothing." Earl put Nikki down because Diamond was right, she wasn't his daughter and there was nothing he could do about it. He looked at her with so much pain in his eyes and walked out the door. When Earl got outside all of Diamond's little friends were sitting outside by one of their cars with the music blasting, finishing their bottle of Grey Goose.

"Ah, look," one of the guys said. "Here comes Diamond's punk ass boyfriend." The guy that was in Nikki's room walked over to where Earl was standing. Earl wasn't the one for any drama and wasn't in the mood. He tried to get into his car.

"Oh, what's up little homey? Did Diamond put you out too?"

"Man, don't you have something better to do?" The guy drew back and punched Earl in the side of his face. Earl knew how to fight; he just wasn't a fighter. He hit the guy back and knocked him to the ground with two punches. Earl had so much frustration built up inside of him that he took it all out on the guy. When he hit the ground, Earl began to kick him in the face. The guy's friends saw what was going on and ran to help him. One of the guys grabbed Earl and Earl hit him in the mouth and the other guys all jumped in. Earl was hanging with them until he was hit in the head with the vodka bottle. He staggered and was hit in the side of his face and was dazed. The next thing you know, everything went bad. All six of the guys jumped Earl and beat him badly. Diamond came outside to smoke a Basic cigarette and saw what was going on. She ran over and started yelling, smacking all of them and trying to pull them off Earl. She got them to stop, and they all ran and got into their cars and pulled off. Earl was bleeding ferociously, and he wasn't moving. Diamond ran in the house and called 9-1-1. She called his cousins also.

Earl was hospitalized, he had two broken ribs, a broken nose, a fractured right arm, a black eye and a mild concussion. Diamond tried to visit him, but Earl wanted nothing to do with her. When she got to the hospital, she and Earl's cousins got into an altercation, and she was escorted out by security. Rosetta no longer allowed her to see Nikki and had nothing to do with her either. Diamond went home to her lonely apartment where she stayed for the next week, she didn't want to be bothered with anyone. She tried calling Earl on several occasions, but he told Mama Rita not to give him any calls from her and when he answered the phone, he would just hang up. After about a month of the same routine, Diamond's feelings were truly hurt. Earl acted as if he didn't even recognize her voice anymore and she figured two can play that game; he wanted to dog her, although it was her fault, she was going to make him really have a reason to hate her. She started messing with his best friend, she knew this was dirty, but she thought "*it's a dirty game, but somebody's got to do it.*"

Dre, Earl's best friend, had gone out of town for several weeks training for a job and was unaware of what had happened to his boy. He went to Diamond's house looking for him. When Diamond came to the door, she was a little scared to open it because everyone wanted to beat her ass for playing a dirty game and she knew her day was coming.

"What's up, Dre?," Diamond asked through the locked screen door.

"Nothing, where is my boy?" Diamond sighed with relief; he didn't know. Diamond let him in.

"So, where have you been? I haven't seen your fine ass in a minute."

"I'm tired of this same old atmosphere. I needed something different, so I went to North Carolina to look for me a place and train for this new job paying like sixty G's a year."

"I know that's right because I'm tired of being here too. I hate it here." Diamond and Dre talked for about half an hour and then he interrupted.

"So, where is my boy?"

"Oh, we're not together anymore."

"Damn, what happened?" She started with her fake crying.

"He don't want me anymore. He won't even talk to me." Dre gave her a one-handed hug and she wrapped her arms around his neck and cried even harder on his shoulder.

"Man, what happened?" Diamond looked him in his eyes and held her stare.

"I don't know," she whispered as she softly kissed his lips. Dre pushed her away from him.

"Hey, that's my dude and he love you too much for me to play him like that."

"Your dude has someone else. He won't even talk to me, and you know I always liked you."

"I'm sorry things didn't work out between the two of you, but I can't play my boy like this." Diamond began to rub his manhood. It had been several weeks for them both and she felt him beginning to harden. He closed his eyes but then realized what he was doing and shook off the temptation. Diamond started to lick around his ear and his neck and once again he let down his guard. She unzipped his pants, dropped to her knees and proceeded to perform oral sex. Dre took a couple of steps backward and ran into the couch, so he sat down. Diamond had him squeezing his eyes shut, his toes curled up and when he came, she swallowed every drop of his cum and continued to suck his limp manhood until it hardened again. She took off all her clothes, sat on his lap with her back to him and put him inside of her. They sexed each other for at least an hour, and she let him hit it any way he wanted to, and she came three times. No one had ever hit it, put her in the positions or made her scream like he had, not even Tyron. This was one dick that she was going to keep.

CHAPTER - 9

Dre didn't really like or want Diamond as a girl, but the sex was nothing like he had ever had. He didn't have a girlfriend, so he continued to sleep with her. She wanted to keep him around for the sex and to get back at Earl for hurting her feelings. After a month of almost everyday sex, Diamond became pregnant with twins and there was no doubt in her mind that they were Dre's. For the first time in a long time, he was the only guy she was sleeping with. Dre wasn't trying to hear that; he didn't have any kids and wasn't ready for any. He knew Diamond was a "rat" and he didn't want to be stuck with her.

"Man, you need to go and take care of that." Dre told Diamond.

"What do you mean?" Diamond asked distraughtly.

"An abortion or something. I'll pay for it. I don't want any kids and that'll break Earl's heart."

"First of all, I don't believe in abortions. Second of all, if you didn't want any kids then you should have strapped up."

"You told me you had that three-year thing."

"Oh well and third of all, I don't care about how Earl feels. He should have stayed around if he wanted to be with me or didn't want me with anyone else."

"You are a dirty bitch."

"Somebody's gotta do it." Dre got his things and left. He couldn't believe he had gotten himself mixed up with a scandalous bitch like Diamond.

The next morning, Dre brought over a pregnancy test, stood in the bathroom and watched her take the test. Sure, enough it was positive.

"Fuck!," he yelled and left. He went over Earl's, who had bought himself a nice house, to tell him the bad news. He

would rather he heard it from him than hear it on the street. Earl was hurt but he didn't want to show his emotions. He shook his head.
"Man, you know we're not going to let a female come between us," Dre said.
"Man, I can see if you just fucked her but damn, you got her pregnant. I'm going to need some time to think about this. You can go ahead and see yourself out." Dre respected Earl's wishes and left.

Diamond wasn't as happy as she thought she would be because she really wanted Earl back. She figured since it was his best friend, she did have a part of him, but Dre didn't really come to see her as much as he used to. He'd call to check on the babies and he'd still sleep with her because he didn't want anyone else nutting on his baby's head, but that was the light of it. Once again, Diamond became bored and started kicking it. She would smoke weed, occasionally, with Tyron and get drunk on her lonely nights. Diamond really started to pick up a lot of weight and became depressed. When she reached her second trimester, Dr. Reed put her on bed rest because of complications of preeclampsia - or high blood pressure - but she didn't listen. She still hung out with Tyron and getting high, drinking and continuously having rough sex. Tyron didn't have a fear of hitting it because he knew she was already pregnant.

One morning, she woke up around 3 o'clock in the morning because she was cramping bad, so she went to the bathroom and her panties were soaked with blood. She called her mother to take her to the emergency room, but Rosetta had had it with her and refused to answer the phone. She called Dre five times, but he didn't answer either. She was afraid to call Tyron, so she called Earl and just so happen, he was on vacation. Earl still loved Diamond, he just didn't want her and didn't like her dirty ways. He took her to the hospital and was by her side the entire time. She lost her babies, a boy and a girl, and tried to patch things up with Earl but he had let his last tear fall over her. He dropped her off back at her house and went about his way. Earl did tell Dre that Diamond had lost the babies, he was happier than a child on Christmas day and went on about his way, too.

CHAPTER - 10

Diamond had burned too many bridges and was alone, struggling to raise her one-year-old son, Brandon. Her friend Erica, who lived in the next complex, was tired of her complaining and always trying to be underneath her, so every time her boyfriend, Rob would call from prison, she would let Diamond talk to his best friend. He had gotten eight years but was about to be released after serving three years for robbery and selling drugs. His name is Vonte' and he had six more months before being released on good behavior. He and Diamond became good phone buddies, and he began to call her every day until her phone was disconnected, then they started writing every week but that wasn't enough, so Diamond got a phone turned on in Nikki's name: ghetto! Their conversations were so intense that she really started to fall for him; he seemed to be a good person who just made some bad decisions in life.

When Vonte' was released, he went to his mother's house in Phoenix, Arizona and when Diamond received her welfare check, she sent Vonte' a bus ticket so he could come and stay with her temporarily. A week later, they were in love and the temporary stay became permanent. Vonte' was trying to get a job and do the right thing because he didn't want to go back to jail, that was a vacation he did not enjoy. He tried to get a job at factories and small companies, but of course, no one wants to hire a convict, so he settled at McDowell's. He didn't really have to pay any bills because Diamond was on housing. She didn't have to pay any rent and she received food stamps and a utility check, so his money was just extra. Vonte' worked two months and then Diamond became pregnant. She started to bug him by calling him at work all day stating that she needed him to come home because she was either ill, lonely, horny, or hungry, just any excuse to get him home and eventually, he was fired. Diamond felt it was her fault that Vonte lost his job, so she went to 'Food City', a grocery store and applied for a job and was hired on the spot. She worked four hours a day, twenty hours a week since she was part-time and couldn't even do that. She was rude to the customers and would stand at her register texting Vonte' and anybody else that would text her back and eventually, she was fired, too.

Like any other "M-A-N", Vonte' didn't like being broke so he went back to what he was used to: the street life. He tried to move anything movable: weight, weed, CD's, TV's whatever and even started using stolen checks, until he was given a tap on the wrist with house arrest for ninety days. That was fine with him because he used the time to make Diamond's house, "The Spot." Diamond was bringing him most of his cliental. She knew who smoked marijuana and cocaine. The operation was great, they were making anywhere from five hundred to two-thousand dollars a night Everyone knew to come to the back door including the police. Vonte' started noticing customers he had never seen before, but he was being greedy, so he just let it go.

A month later Diamond's apartment was raided, and she was later evicted. At the time of the raid, luckily, Vonte' was waiting on a shipment and all they found was a scale and some marijuana residue in the ashtray, and of course, "he had a habit" so part of his probation was to go to Drug Awareness meetings three times a week for thirty days and that was nothing to him because it sure beat going back to jail. Vonte' took four thousand dollars out of his secret hiding place, in Brandon's closet in a hole in the wall that the police didn't find during the raid, and put down the security deposit, which was the first and last month's rent on an apartment. He paid their rent for six months and went and got a job at another fast-food restaurant. Although he had a nice stash put away, he was trying to make a 'good look' for his probation officer plus, he wanted more money before his first child was born because he wanted to be able to do for his child. That raid had him scared shitless, so he decided he was done with the drug game for good.

Vonte' bought a new cell phone and told Diamond not to call him during his work hours, not even on his cell phone unless it was a major emergency, otherwise, he wasn't coming to the phone. She tried to call one time.
"Hey baby. Are you busy because I miss you?"
"What did I tell you?"
"I know baby..."
"Are you in labor?," Vonte' interrupted.
"No but..." Vonte' hung up the phone and asked his manager not to give him any more calls. That was the end of that.

Vonte' nor Diamond had their driver's license, but he wanted to buy her a car. He was used to catching the bus, but he knew it was already hard to get around on the bus with one child and now that she would have two, it would really be a task. He didn't like her standing at the bus stop in all that heat, but he didn't want her to know he had money put away either, because she always found a way to spend it, so he waited until his third paycheck, which was only one hundred eighty-nine dollars and twenty cents, but Diamond didn't know. He added the needed money and bought Diamond a nice ride. It was a red 2005 Chrysler Sebring that he had tint put on the windows, some rims and added a sound system. His babies were going to be rolling in style! He loved Diamond and his unborn child and did his best to show it.

November twenty first, a few days before Thanksgiving, Diamond and Vonte' had a seven pounds, nine ounces and 19 inches long little boy who they named Vonte' Ray Junior and he was a spitting image of his father. This was the first time that there wasn't any doubt in Diamond's mind as to who her baby's father was and it felt great. Diamond was finally ready to settle down and get married and so was Vonte'.

CHAPTER - 11

Diamond decided that she wanted to come clean about every secret that she felt Vonte' should know about. She was laying in her hospital bed and Vonte' was sitting in the chair next to her bed playing with his first and only beautiful son. She was just smiling as she watched because this was the first time she'd experienced a father, a real father, for her child.

"Sweetheart, there's something very important that I need to talk to you about," Diamond said in a soft, loving voice.

"Anything baby, just let me know what's on your mind," he said as he kissed Vonte' Jr.

"The real reason that I couldn't have the baby natural is because I have herpes." If he wanted to leave her after finding out her secret, she'd preferred it was now while she had medication and supervision. He looked up from his son and gave her a distraught look.

"And we've been doing it without a rubber for over a year and you're just telling me this?" Vonte' got up and put his son in the hospital bassinet.

"Baby, I wanted to tell you, but I didn't know how, I didn't want you to judge me and leave me."

"Diamond, I love you. You just gave birth to my first son, and you took me in when I had no place to go. I look at you as a goddess, and now, you're telling me that you've been lying to me for over a year?"

"I have been taking every precaution so you wouldn't catch it. The nights that I didn't want to have sex and I just gave you head for a couple of days; I wasn't bleeding all those times; I was protecting you." Vonte' sat there silent, just thinking. Diamond had begun to cry because she loved Vonte' and she didn't want to betray him. Vonte's eyes filled with tears, he got up and left the room. As he was leaving, Diamond called out his name.

"Vonte'?" He turned to look at her.
"I love you." He turned away as he continued to walk out.

Vonte' went outside and freaked two Black-n-Milds, smoked them both, and went to the hospital cafeteria and had himself a cup of black coffee. An hour later, he returned to Diamond's room where she had cried herself to sleep. Diamond had sent Vonte' Jr. to the nursery and had asked the nurse for some pain pills, because not only did her stitches hurt, but so did her heart. Vonte' went to retrieve his son and waited two hours for Diamond to wake up and when she saw Vonte's face, she began to cry all over again because she thought he was gone forever. Vonte' walked over to Diamond's bed and kissed her on the lips.
"I love you too, baby. I trust you and I don't think that you would hurt me. You have given me something that no other girl has, and I will love you forever for that. I don't care about you having herpes, people live with that every day, I read up on all the STD's when I was in prison. Are you on some kind of medication?"
"Yes," Diamond answered.
"Are you taking them like you're supposed to?"
"Yes, I have been since I found out."
"Alright, everything will be fine. Don't worry about that."
Diamond closed her eyes and said a silent prayer, thanking God for letting her find a man that she would love forever because he loved her for who she is. Diamond was in the hospital for two more days and when she returned home, she almost had a heart attack. She didn't have a baby shower because she didn't have that many friends and her family didn't too much fool with her, so while she was in the hospital, Vonte' bought his son everything that he thought he needed and decorated his little room in sports: the lamp shade, border, bumper pads and bedding all matched, he even bought Diamond a rocking chair and sat it in the corner of the baby's

room. From that point on, Vonte' was the man that she was going to marry.

Diamond had called Rosetta and made things right with her before she went to the hospital to have Vonte Jr., she apologized for everything that she had done wrong in the past and Rosetta kept Brandon until her stitches healed. Rosetta allowed her to spend more time with Nikki, but she wouldn't let her stay too long because she wasn't too fond of Vonte'. He was a good guy who treated her daughter like gold, but he had been to prison for many years, and she just didn't trust a man with little girls. She wasn't sure if he and Diamond were really going to be together and she didn't want all of those different men around her granddaughter. Diamond understood and was alright with her decisions as long as she could see her every day.

CHAPTER - 12

A couple of months had passed and Vonte' started noticing weird things going on with Diamond, she'd wake up in cold sweats screaming, she had laid Vonte Jr. down in a box and couldn't find him until he began to cry, and he found her asleep completely nude behind the bathroom door on the floor. He thought she was doing drugs, so he took her to the emergency room where they kept her overnight and found no drugs in her system. Vonte' quit his job because something was going on with his woman, he didn't feel comfortable leaving his children alone with her anymore and weird things continued to happen.

Vonte' finally took Diamond to see Dr. Floyd to have her evaluated and she was treated for schizophrenia. Dr. Floyd showed her pictures of items and asked her to identify them, and she saw some crazy things and was diagnosed as being bipolar with affective disorder manic, severe degree without mention of psychotic behavior. The voices that she heard continued to tell her to do bad things, so she was put on Social Security and given eleven hundred dollars a month, but she had to wait a few months before she received her first check. Diamond no longer had to worry about working. Vonte' had used up all his savings by keeping the bills current, since it was his fault Diamond no longer received housing assistance and she only received $450 a month from welfare for her three kids, plus food stamps. She gave Rosetta a portion of that for Nikki, so Vonte' went back to what he knew best, being a stick-up kid. He couldn't see his woman and children struggling, sitting in the dark, or better yet, homeless, and without air conditioning in this hot city, you would probably have a heat stroke, so he did what he had to do.

Vonte' was breaking into people's houses stealing whatever he could: televisions, DVD's, video games, movies, camcorders, cameras, whatever, and he only sold them to people he knew. He was making enough money to keep all the bills up and he was never gone more than two to three hours a day. Diamond was alright with what he was doing because her man was home majority of the time.

Although Diamond had her man, she became very depressed and didn't understand why. She began to pick up a lot of weight, then she missed her period. Vonte' loved her and their children, but they were not financially able to take care of any more children. Diamond went to the local corner store and put a pregnancy test into her purse, asked to use their public restroom and took the test. It came up positive. Diamond went to Dr. Reed's and was three months pregnant.
"Look, Diamond, I'm not trying to go back to jail. I'm about to go and find me a job."
"What are we going to do about this month's rent?," Diamond asked.
"We'll take your three seventy-five and apply it toward the rent and we'll sell half of your food stamps. That'll give us five hundred and fifty."
"OK, we're still a hundred dollars short, plus we have to pay the utilities, Vonte' Jr. needs diapers and both of the kid's shoes are too small."
"Damn it! Go buy Lil' Vonte' some diapers and fill up the gas tank with the other seventy-five dollars from your check, but that's going to leave us broke until next month unless your check comes." Diamond gave Vonte' a sad look.
"What do you want me to do? I'm trying."
"You said you were the man of the house, and you would take care of things."
"Let's just hope your check gets here by the first of the month. You can't ask your mom?"

“I don’t want to ask her. The last time we were in a bind, I had to hear about it for two months, and I’m tired of depending on her. She already takes care of Nikki and ever since she found out that I’m pregnant again, she’s been acting funny.” Vonte' went out that day and applied for every job he saw with a ‘Now Hiring’ sign. He went to temporary agencies, and small businesses, but no one wanted to hire a young black man who had been to prison all his adult life, had no previous experience and a rap sheet an arm’s length.

Vonte' continued with what he was doing, petty theft, but this time, he went a step further by using one of the checks he had stolen from a house. He had Diamond fill it out and sign it and he took it to a check cashing place around the corner where they charged him fourteen dollars to cash a four-hundred- and seventy-five-dollar check. They paid their rent and gas bill. Diamond had sold some of her food stamps so they would be alright for the month. Vonte' was hoping that Diamond would receive her Social Security check the following month, but they looked in the mailbox every day for the first week and nothing. Diamond started nagging Vonte' about the money again.

Vonte’ did another break-in and as he was pulling away from the house, the owner returned home. He had cased the house and thought he knew this lady’s schedule, but she was feeling a little sick that day and decided to go home early. The lady looked at the license plate, the make and model of the car because this was a quiet neighborhood where everyone knew everyone, and she had never seen this person before. When the lady got out of her car and walked to her side door, she noticed it was ajar. She ran to the end of the driveway, but the red Sebring was gone. She ran back up her driveway and was afraid to go inside her own home, so she went to the neighbors, but they weren’t there so she walked to the pay phone and called the police. The police arrived at the lady's house in about ten minutes. She gave them a description of the car and the numbers on the license plate that she could remember. They went inside of the house together and noticed her Sony television, DVD/VCR player, some DVD's, some CD's, her 24-karat gold watch, two 14 karat rings, a digital camera, a camcorder and a few of her checkbooks were missing. The officer took the report and called it in.

Vonte' went home and gave Diamond the watch, the rings and the DVD/VCR player and sold the television set to one of Diamond's friends. As they were on their way to drop off the camcorder to one of his boy's houses, the police pulled them over for expired tags and Vonte' was caught with the lady's checks, the camcorder, and some CD's and they both were arrested. Diamond was released, but they kept Vonte' and he was charged with the other robberies because of the other stolen checks that he had used to help with their bills. Diamond was put on a forty-five-day house arrest for being an accomplice and violating her probation. Vonte' was given the rest of his sentence, four years, that he had before he met Diamond. He would never get to see his second child born.

As usual, Diamond couldn't tolerate being alone, so she called her friend, Tamika every day inquiring about what she was doing and keeping her away from her man, Chris, for her to spend time with her. Chris grew tired of Tamika always being gone and she began to miss her man.
"Look, Diamond, I can't continue to be here day in and day out. My son enjoys playing with your kids, but I do have a man at home and with us always being gone, it's beginning to cause problems at home."
"Girl, y'all too much in love to have problems."
"Yeah and we're so in love because we take care of each other."

"Well, I need to find me a man so that we can take care of each other. I'm tired of being cooped up in this house all day with these kids."
"Why don't you go get a job or something?"
"I tried that, and it didn't work, plus nobody's going to hire me. I have a felony, and I don't have nobody to watch my kids."
"You can always put them in daycare."
"Please, two kids in daycare, you know how much that will cost? That'll be my whole months check and I'm pregnant, so I'm going to need to be off in like five months, so I might as well just stay at home."
"You can always go to welfare and get help."
"I'm good. I get over two G's a month to stay at home and watch my own kids. I need some other way to occupy my time."
"What happened to all of your jellies?"
"They're played out. Man, I need something new. Somebody that everybody don't know."
"Hmmm..."
"What?"
"I'm thinking... my dude's boy just got out of prison, but I don't know if you want to talk to him or not."
"Why not?"
"Well, he went to jail for attempted murder."
"Oh, so he's a thug? Just my type of man! I need a man who can fuck me real hard in some Timberland boots."
"You are one sick individual."
"I know, that's why the boys, the boys they love me." They both began to laugh.
"How about this Friday? You come over and we can play some spades and have a few drinks?"
"I don't want to drag these kids out. Why don't y'all come over here, that way, if I like him, y'all can just leave him here."

"You are so nasty."
"I know. So, what time on Friday?"
"I'll let you know."

Diamond cleaned her house every day until Friday, so she wouldn't have that much to do. Friday morning, Diamond woke up early, and cooked a big breakfast: pancakes, sausage links, scrambled eggs and cheesy grits. She cleaned up again and went to the grocery store for chips and dip, pop, beer and some more breakfast food, just in case Chris' s friend stayed the night. She gave her kids a bath and dressed them in nice pajamas and burned a few musk incenses. She ordered two large pepperoni pizzas, took a shower, added her Love Spell lotion by Victoria's Secret, put on a pair of low-rider blue jeans and a yellow tank top and waited for her guests.

Tamika was right on time, as usual, her son Mark, Chris and Rashod all arrived at 7:05 PM and ironically, Rashod was wearing a pair of Timberlands. He was tall, dark-skinned, a body out of this world, brush cut with deep waves and was dressed in some black jean shorts that he had sagging and a tan Polo shirt that matched his Timberlands. Diamond didn't care that he had just done eight years, she was ready to get with him right then. She didn't even want to play spades anymore. She wanted Tamika and her family to leave so that she could spend the time that she had dreamed about the last couple of days with Rashod, but she kept her cool. She didn't want to come off too easy and scare him away. She had to come up with a plan to get him to stay without sounding like a ho. They played spades and they were partners, so she was able to talk to him and get to know him. After the first game, all of the beer was gone, so Diamond asked Tamika and Chris to run to the liquor store, while lil' Vonte was asleep, and Brandon and Mark were upstairs playing then she wouldn't have anyone in her way.

Once Diamond had Rashod alone, she started sizing him up and changed the CD from Weezy to Jodeci. She seductively walked over to the chair that Rashod was sitting in, rubbing her hands across his chest. She moved behind him and massaged his shoulders.

"So how long has it been since you've been with a woman?," Diamond asked.

Rashod chuckled.

"Why?"

"I'm asking the questions here."

"Oh, that's how you do it?"

"Naw." Diamond answered as she walked around the chair. "This is how I do it." She kissed him in the mouth. He followed suit and kissed her back. To Rashod, Diamond wasn't that bad looking, she had her own crib, appeared to be neat and about her business. Diamond hurdled over him, as she slowly unbuttoned his shorts, she stroked his manhood until she got a reaction. Once it was good and hard, she dropped to her knees and gave him her specialty. When she felt him squirming in his chair and grabbing her head, she stopped.

"Stay the night with me?," Diamond asked. Rashod pushed her head back between his legs.

"Baby, don't stop," Rashod moaned. Diamond licked his head.

"Are you going to stay the night with me?" He continued to ignore her question, so she went back to work until he busted in her mouth. She continued to please him until he pushed too hard on the chair trying to get away because Diamond had put it on him, and he couldn't handle it. The chair fell backwards, and he caught himself on the wall. She got up wiping her mouth and smiling.

"So, are you going to stay so I can give you the real deal?"

"That wasn't the real deal?," Rashod asked as he wiped the sweat from his forehead.
Diamond began to laugh.
"Oh, that was nothing."
"I'll think about it," Rashod said while smiling. Diamond walked toward him and grabbed his still erect penis. "OK, OK I'll stay, damn. I see I'm going to have to turn these tables because you're not going to have me in check, especially not on the first day that we met." Just as Rashod was fixing his clothes, Tamika and Chris walked into the house with a bottle of Grey Goose vodka and a liter of cranberry juice.
"Oh, I see y'all slowed things down a little bit," Tamika said.
"What are you talking about?," Diamond asked looking guilty.
"This music that you're playing. What's wrong with you?" Tamika knew something had happened because Diamond was acting weird.
"Nothing, shit. I need a drink, y'all took forever."
"You're the one that sent us all the way to the liquor store knowing it's the first of the month and everybody and their momma was in there. You can't have a drink! Did you forget, you're pregnant?" Diamond laughed as she looked at Rashod waiting for a reaction or a response, which she never got. Rashod couldn't keep his eyes off her the rest of the evening. He couldn't believe that he'd known this girl for less than three hours and he was feeling her. Diamond danced and was grinding in her chair all night and that kept Rashod turned on imagining how the sex would be if the head was that good.
"Well Diamond, it's getting late. We're going to be getting out of here," Tamika said. Diamond didn't mind because she was ready for them to go when they first got there.
"Alright, I'm about ready to chill out too. Ain't no telling what those kids are upstairs doing. Rashod are you ready?," Tamika asked.
Diamond put her hands on her hips and stared at Rashod. He looked up at her and began to laugh.

"Naw, y'all go ahead, I'm going to stay here and chill for a while. I'll find a way home," he said. Tamika looked at Diamond with a "wow" look. Diamond gave her a wink and smiled. Tamika went upstairs and got Mark's jacket on, and they left.

"Man, Tamika, what's up with your girl? She just met Rashod not even three hours ago and he's ready to chill with her already?," Chris asked.

"That's my girl and one thing about her, she has no problem getting what she wants."

"I guess, but isn't she still with her baby's dad? The one that just went to jail?"

"Dude has four years! What do you expect her to do?"

"Wait."

"Yeah, right."

"So, if I got a four-year stretch, you wouldn't wait on me?"

"I guess you'll never know until it happens. Which it bet not," Tamika said while punching
Chris' shoulder. Diamond ran upstairs.

"I'll be right back, let me go check on my kids." Lil' Vonte' was on the floor asleep and Brandon was still up playing.

"Come on baby, you should've been in the bed." She got him up and put him to bed. She picked Lil' Vonte up, changed his diaper and put him to bed, too. She went into the bathroom, freshened up and returned to her date, who had made himself at home. He had cleaned up the table in the kitchen, made himself a drink and was sitting in the living room watching television. She took a seat beside Rashod on the couch for a moment, she moved closer to him and began to massage his chest.

"I see you must work out a lot."

"Yeah, eight years is a long time. I had nothing but time to stay in the gym and read. I took up a couple of trades and hopefully within the next few weeks, I can get myself a job or something."

"Well, if you need somewhere to stay until you get on your feet, you can always stay here."

"I'll keep that in mind, but I've had shackles on my feet for too long, I need some freedom for a while."

"We'll see if things change after tonight. I got you to spend the night with me didn't I?"

Rashod laughed. Diamond moved even closer and began to massage his manhood. He rested his head on the back of the couch as She proceeded to unbutton his shorts so she could give him some more of her good loving. She didn't want him to cum, she just wanted to get him there. Once he began to moan, Diamond pushed mute on the remote to silence the television, she grabbed the remote to her stereo system and put in a slow but freaky rap CD and began to strip. She slowly took off her yellow tank top while she slowly danced to the music. She turned around and faced the wall so that he could see how her "boy shorts" were holding up her butt. She shook it as she bent over and touched her toes then proceeded to take off her shorts. Now she stood in front of him newborn naked. Rashod was amazed at her body; she had two kids that he knew about and had recently learned that she was now pregnant. She had a few stretch marks and a small pouch, but she still looked good.

"Where is your kids' father, because I'm not in the mood for any drama? I'm still on probation."

"Baby, you don't have nothing to worry about but satisfying me. My kid's dad is locked up, but I don't want to think about him right now." Diamond walked over to Rashod and seductively kissed him in the mouth. She hurdled over him and took off his Polo shirt, he laid back and let her take charge. Diamond pulled his black shorts off over his boots because it was something about guys in Timberlands with her and she wanted him to have her while he was wearing nothing but his boots. She hurdled back over him and began to ride him slow and seductively. For the past couple of days, Rashod had been with the girl he was with before he went to prison and Diamond's little seduction wasn't really phasing him. She looked him in his eyes, and it looked as if he wasn't enjoying her, so she picked up the pace. She began to ride him faster and harder, tightening her muscles on his erect penis. Rashod's eyes closed tightly, his head rested on the back of the couch again and he began to claw at her body. Diamond knew she had him, they sexed each other for the next hour all over the house until they made it to her bedroom where they fell asleep with Rashod still inside of her.

The next morning, Diamond woke up, fed her kids and put them in front of the television to watch cartoons. She made Rashod breakfast in bed. She fed him strawberries as he ate his pancakes, sausages and scrambled eggs. After they finished their meal, Rashod felt as if Diamond was one that he would keep around, so he was going to go ahead and turn her out. He performed oral sex on her, and he made her cum so many times that she began to cry because it felt so good. He stuck in the head of his penis and teased her until she came again. Once she started squirming around the bed, pulling the sheets and begging him to stop, he began to sex her very hard and rough until she was screaming at the top of her lungs.
"I'm running this show now. This is mine and you bet not give it to nobody. Do you hear me?"
"Yes," Diamond screamed. She couldn't do anything but agree. She never had anyone sex her like this and she had been with many, many men, but none of them ever pleased her so well that they made her cry.
"You said your dude was doing a four-year bid, so there is no reason for anybody to be around you, do you understand?"
"Yes." Rashod began to hit it even harder.
"No, do you understand me?"
"Yes baby, I promise, I will never give your pussy away."
"Don't play with me."

"As long as you give me this good loving, you'll never have to worry about me." Rashod finished up and took a nap. She laid there staring at the ceiling and couldn't believe that after one night, this dude actually had her wrapped around his finger. She didn't want him to ever leave. Diamond rolled over and put her arm around his chest and fell asleep with her new man.

CHAPTER - 13

"Diamond, why don't you get up and make me some breakfast?," Rashod asked.

"Baby, I'm tired, the baby has been moving around all night, so I didn't get that much sleep and I planned on sleeping in today. The kids are with my mom for the weekend because I'm supposed to be resting."

"Well, I'm hungry. What am I supposed to do while you rest?"

"Go and get a bowl of cereal or put some waffles in the toaster. Better yet, why don't you make us both some breakfast?"

"Man, I don't live here, and I don't know where all your stuff is."

"I can tell you."

"Well, while you're using all of this energy to try to teach me something, you might as well go do it yourself."

"Fine." Diamond got out of bed and made Rashod some breakfast and took it upstairs to the bedroom. She didn't make herself anything because her contractions were so bad and close that she didn't feel like eating. She tried taking a nap but was in so much pain that she asked Rashod to take her to the hospital. He had a red 1986 Brougham Cadillac with red tinted windows, red leather seats, Cadillac rims, a booming system and a fifth wheel on the back. Diamond had seen that car before but didn't know where. This was not a car you saw every day and she remembered it so well because it is an original, but she never had seen who the driver was. Rashod got up, went to his car and got his overnight pouch, went into the bathroom and brushed his teeth, shaved, took a shower and then got dressed in a white Nike jogging suit.

"Come on, Rashod. My contractions are only five minutes apart."

"Here I come, let me polish my shoes right quick." He cleaned his white Nike's, put them on and looked in the mirror to make sure he was crisp and clean. Diamond was lying on the couch in tears.

"Are you ready?" Rashod asked as if Diamond was the one taking all day. She didn't even answer; she just got up and grabbed the bag she had prepared for the hospital and went and stood by his car door waiting for him to let her in. Rashod got on the expressway and drove like a maniac, he hit every pothole he approached, he was swerving in and out of lanes and Diamond couldn't wait to get out of that car, but she didn't complain. By the time she was admitted, her contractions were two minutes apart. The nurses got her prepared and Rashod left because "he had something to do." She was in labor for six hours before she gave birth to another boy. He was eight pounds, nine ounces and 21 inches long and she named him Deontae' Ray.

The five days that she was in the hospital Rashod, came to visit her once. She missed Vonte' and wished he could have seen his second child born but she didn't really cry because she had prepared herself to be alone. She needed the rest because she already knew it was going to be hard being a single parent of three: a newborn, a one-and-a-half-year-old and a three-year-old. It didn't look like Rosetta was going to give her back Nikki, so she didn't have that to worry about. Now, if she could just get Rashod to help her take care of her three boys then she would be good to go. He had a nice Cadi, he dressed nice, so he had to have some dough and Diamond was going to do what she had to do to make him her new baby daddy until her real baby daddy came home.

Rashod came and picked Diamond up from the hospital as she instructed because he had her house keys and was staying there while she was in the hospital. As soon as she opened the door, the scent of garbage grabbed her nose. She proceeded into the kitchen where she noticed garbage tumbled onto the floor. The trash can was overflowing with beer bottles, chicken boxes, McDowell's wrappers and cigar residue.

"What the hell went on over here?," Diamond asked in an upset voice.

"Oh, a couple of my boys came over and chilled with me, is that alright?" Rashod asked with a smile, while rubbing her back.

"Whatever, will you just clean that up? I don't want my baby inhaling that stinky shit."

"Alright, I'll do it when I get back. I have to make a run real quick."

Diamond ignored the mess and went upstairs to her room knowing that Rashod would clean up his mess. She laid down and got some rest but was awaken by a bunch of loud rap music. She eased out of bed and opened her bedroom door to a face full of smoke. She rolled her eyes and listened while shaking her head. She heard a bunch of guys laughing and talking. She went closer to the bottom of the stairs and listened again when she heard Rashod telling his friends how he had a free ride, that Diamond loved him and would do whatever he said. Diamond went back upstairs and began to cry because she was beginning to miss Vonte', he was the only one who she felt ever really loved her besides Earl. Diamond laid there for another twenty minutes trying to get her thoughts together and then said: "*fuck this bullshit, this is my damn house.*" She got up out of bed, put on a pair of gray jogging pants and a red t-shirt and went downstairs. First, she turned off the stereo and then went into the kitchen where the guys were playing dominoes.

"Excuse me, do y'all mind? I did just have a baby not even a week ago. I'm tired. Shit, don't y'all have somewhere else to hang out?" One of the guys laughed and looked at Rashod,

who felt embarrassed because he had just got done talking trash about how he had her wrapped around his finger.
"Man, Diamond, why don't you gone back to bed with that bullshit," Rashod said.
"No, why don't you and your sorry ass friends go find something to do. It's Tuesday and two o'clock in the afternoon. Don't y'all have a job or something worthwhile to do?"
"You don't need to worry about if I have a job or not," one of the guys said. Diamond looked at Rashod and raised her eyebrows. He already knew that she was about to act up.
"Hold up dogg, this is my girl and I'm the only one that can talk to her like that."
"Man, that's not your main chick anyway. Why are you defending her?"
"Because man, you're not going to disrespect her in her own house. She does have a point; we can go to your spot and let her get some rest."
"Naw man, my girl ain't going for that."
"Alright bro', what about you?," Rashod asked his other friend.
"Man, you know I stay with my mom, and she definitely won't go for it."
"Well, what in the hell makes you think that I would?" Diamond asked.
"Well, I figured since..."
"Man, save it," interrupted Rashod. "Y'all go ahead, I'm going to get the baby and let her get some rest. I'll holla at y'all tomorrow." Diamond was surprised and gave his friends an evil smile, turned around and proceeded upstairs.
"Man, I thought you said that you were running things around here?," his friend asked.
"Boy, get outta here. She's right why aren't you at work?"
"I lost my job a couple of months ago, but that's a whole 'nother story. We are gon' go and let you playhouse. We'll

catch up with you later. When you're done playing daddy," his friend said under his breath. Rashod pushed him out of the house.

"Don't be mad because you're still living in your mama's basement, still putting your name on the Kool-Aid."

"Man, fuck you. I only put my name on the stuff that I buy."

Rashod began to laugh.

"Naw, that's alright, I have somebody to do that. Shit, give her a week to heal." Rashod's friend left, he went upstairs and got the baby as he promised and let Diamond rest for the remainder of the day. He cleaned up his mess and rested on the couch. He made hamburger and French fries and, of course, she pleased him the best way she could before he went to sleep that night.

CHAPTER - 14

A month had passed since Diamond had given birth to Deontae'' and she was ready to kick it. She was still bleeding so sex was out, but she needed to get out of the house. Rashod watched the kids while she went out with Tamika and Erica. For the first time in a long time Diamond wasn't looking for a man because she was actually happy with Rashod. He had his flaws, like everyone, but for the most part, he turned out to be an alright dude. He took her and her kids out to dinner once a week, took the kids to the park on occasions to give her five minutes to herself and she felt herself falling in love with another man. She promised Vonte' and herself that she would never let this happen because she loved Vonte', but he was gone for four years and although she was mostly to blame she felt she still had a life and wasn't going to wait around on him. Vonte' called once a week and they wrote to each other every other day, but Rashod wasn't feeling that.

"Look Diamond, if you're trying to be with me then you're going to have to tell your little boyfriend that you'll talk to him when he gets out. I don't mind him calling once a month to check on the boys because those are his kids but that's enough, and you can write him, but I want to read the letter before it goes into the mail."

"Why? That's my kid's father and we have personal stuff to talk about," Diamond said.

"Do you have anything to hide from me?," Rashod asked.

"No, but I think you're being unfair. I understand that you help me take care of my kids."

"And I take care of you."

"I know and I appreciate that, but you can't try to control me like that. That's like saying you want to listen in on me and my father's conversation."

"Y'all probably don't be talking about nothing, but don't give me any ideas."
"My point exactly, neither do Vonte' and I. With you trying to read my letters, it makes me feel violated."
"Yeah, alright." Rashod dropped the conversation.

One afternoon Diamond had gone to Food City and Rashod was sitting outside on the porch. The mailman walked up and handed him the mail, so he set it on the chair and continued to relax. Rashod became bored and picked up the mail to look at the ads when he noticed a letter from Vonte', at first he just set it back down, but curiosity was killing him, so he picked it back up and observed the envelope.
"I wonder what they be talking about. Is Diamond using me until he comes home? Does she go to visit him?" All kinds of questions came to his mind, so he opened the letter because he knew the things he was writing women when he was locked up. The letter was telling Diamond how much he loved her and the kids, how he couldn't wait to come home to make love to her again, and about how he's going to do it right and marry her when he comes home and so on and so on. Rashod became instantly pissed and knew in his mind that the next time Vonte' called, he was going to answer the phone just to let him know that she does have somebody else now. He tore up the letter and threw it in the neighbor's trash so there would be no evidence. Rashod never mentioned the letter and was going to try to intercept every letter that he wrote her then eventually, if she never wrote back, maybe he would leave her alone.

Rashod had been sleeping on the couch for the past few days because Brandon had been sick, so he and Deontae'' were sleeping with Diamond and there just wasn't enough room for the four of them. He was sleeping well when the telephone rang, he looked at the clock and it read 6:38 AM.

He didn't feel like getting up, so he ignored the phone and rolled back over. The caller hung up and called right back so Rashod got up, grabbed the phone, looked at the caller ID and it was a call from a correctional institute. Rashod smiled as he answered the phone, declined the call and turned the ringer off on the phone. He knew Vonte' had to be hurt, and hopefully he wouldn't call back. Rashod erased the number from the caller ID and went back to sleep.

Every morning, Diamond went to the mailbox looking for a letter from Vonte'. It had been three weeks and she hadn't heard from him, and she just didn't understand. She had written him twice. Actually, he had written her back, she just never received the letters, but Rashod did, and was happy to know that Vonte' knew that she had a "new" man.
Diamond became distraught but instead of getting upset, she used that energy to love Rashod more. Dr. Floyd was helping and so was the medication she was on. After two months of writing Vonte' with no response; she gave up. She was hurt, but what else could she do? She wanted to go visit him, but she was a felon and wasn't allowed at the prison. She went into the living room and laid on Rashod's chest; she needed some reassurance.
"Baby, what are your plans with me?," Diamond asked.
"I plan on giving you the love you deserve. You're a queen and I want to treat you like that. I know you've been through a lot, and I want to make your life better." Diamond kissed his lips.
"You treat me so good, and I appreciate you." She kissed his lips, again and rubbed his muscles. She loved to see him with his shirt off, prison had done him some good. She made love to her man and began to think that she wanted to tell him that she had herpes, but how could she without him getting mad? They had already made love a hundred times, but she wanted to come clean with him and not have any secrets.

Diamond called Tamika, the one who hooked her and Rashod up, and told her how she was in love and wanted to come clean, she asked her to tell him, but she refused to get involved and told her that was something she needed to take care of herself. Diamond thought about it and she was right. Vonte' was alright with it so maybe he will be, too.

On the first of the month when Diamond received her check, she asked Tamika to watch the kids while she and Rashod went to dinner. She took him to Ann's Steak and Crab House and spent close to a hundred dollars.
"Rashod, ever since the day we met, you've made me happy. You're fine, have a sexy body, the sex is great, and you are so good to me and the boys, and I want to thank you. There is something that I want to tell you and I don't want you to be mad at me. I want you to hear everything that I have to say before you say anything."
"What? Your boyfriend coming home?"
"First of all, I don't have a boyfriend, you're the closest thing to a man that I have right now."
"Well, there can't be anything worse than you leaving me."
"Rashod, I have herpes," she said as fast as she could.
"Excuse me?," Rashod asked as if he didn't hear her right.
Diamond looked down to the ground.
"What the fuck did you just say?"
"Rashod, before you trip..."
"Bitch, I've been fucking you without a rubber since the day we met!" Everyone in the restaurant turned and looked at their table.
"Rashod, please lower your voice. You're drawing attention to us."
"I don't give a fuck! You bring me out here with all these damn white folks and bought me this big ole'' fancy dinner to tell me some bullshit like this!"

"Rashod, the only reason I'm telling you is because I love you. I could have taken you on the Maury show."

"Bitch, you can't get rid of that shit."

"I know but..." Rashod threw his drink in her face, got up from the table and flipped over. His eyes filled up with tears.

"Fuck you, man! I'll be by the house to get my shit; better yet, by the time you get home, all my shit will be gone!"

"What do you mean, by the time I get home? I'm leaving with you."

"Like hell you are!" By that time the manager was at their table.

"Ma'am, we're going to have to ask you two to leave," but Rashod was already out the door. "You can pay the bill at the front desk, but you have to leave now." Diamond was crying so hard that she couldn't catch her breath. She paid the bill and went outside and sat on the curb. She called Tamika and asked her to come and pick her up. While she was waiting, she called Rashod and got his voicemail, so she left a message. "Baby, I understand why you're upset, but I wouldn't do anything to hurt you. I'm taking medicine and haven't had an outbreak in almost a year. I just had Deontae' and he is fine. Go and get yourself checked out and it'll prove what I'm saying. Vonte' and I have been sexually active for three years and he doesn't have it. Baby don't leave me because I was trying not to have any secrets with you. I love you and once you understand that you'll be fine baby; come home. I need you and so does the boys." Rashod was already at the clinic, he left the restaurant and went straight there, but it took two days before the results would come back. Rashod rolled past Diamond's house every day, because he wanted to believe her, but he just continued to think, "*what if I have it now*'?" When he saw her outside, all he could do was give her the middle finger. Rashod went back to the girl he was with before he went to jail, the one that had his Cadillac for eight years, the one that kept money on his books, the one that he knew really loved him and was going to be there no matter what, Sonya.

Sonya was about forty years old; her family was pretty wealthy and when her grandfather died he left her a house, a Cadillac, one almost like Rashod's, and a hundred thousand dollars because she was his only grandchild. Sonya and Rashod had been together for three years before he went to jail and although she had "friends," Rashod was her number one. Sonya was smart, she invested some of her money, went to school and got her nursing degree and put some money up for her son, Jeff. Rashod stayed with Sonya for almost a week and Diamond called him every day, five to six times a day, but He would never answer his phone. He received his test results, and they were negative. *Maybe Diamond was telling the truth, he* thought. He waited a couple more days and went to see her.

Rashod pulled into Diamond's driveway at two o'clock in the morning. She and the boys were sound asleep. He used his key, that he never returned, and eased upstairs. He took off his clothes and got into bed with her as quietly as he could, put his arms around her waist and quietly whispered her name. "Diamond, baby, I'm home." She jumped as she opened her eyes, but she didn't move. "I'm sorry I didn't believe you, but that came as a shock to me."
"I told you I would never hurt you," Diamond said.
"I know baby and again, I apologize."
"Is it OK to make love to you or should I wait?" Diamond didn't answer, she rolled over and made love to her man.

CHAPTER - 15

The week that Sonya and Rashod had spent together brought back old feelings, they were once planning on getting married, but that eight-year stretch had put a hold on that. Rashod continued to spend a lot of time with Diamond and her boys, but he started to spend more and more time with Sonya. Sonya took him out of town every other weekend just to get him away from the same everyday routine. She knew about Diamond but wasn't threatened by her because she knew the bond that she and Rashod shared even with all the trials and tribulations, that a bitch would never come between them. He told her almost everything because they were friends first, and that's what kept them so strong.

Diamond started noticing a change in Rashod, he wasn't always there like he used to be, and he developed this "I don't give a fuck" attitude. He'd only stay at her house about three days out of the week and kept saying he was spending more time with his mother, Latifah. He took Diamond over and let her meet Latifah just to shut her up which made Diamond think that she was in there, but Latifah loved Sonya, she was like the daughter she never had. She treated Diamond with respect when she came around, but when she was gone everything was Sonya, Sonya, Sonya. She called Sonya almost every day and even kept Jeff, who called her grandma, so that she and Rashod could go out of town.

One afternoon, Rashod and Diamond were at home watching a boot-leg movie and Sonya called. Diamond was lying on Rashod's chest and tried to see the phone number, but he had it turned so she couldn't see. He hit the ignore button and continued to watch the movie. Twenty minutes later, his phone rang again and this time he answered.

"Hello."
"Hey, sexy. What are you doing?" Diamond sat up and looked at him because she could hear his other woman.
"Nothing, just sitting here watching a movie."
"With her?"
"Man, what's up?"
"Are you coming to see me tonight or does Diamond have you on lock down?"
"Naw, I'll be there later." She gave him a distraught look.
"Oh, will you?," she asked as she got up from the couch. Rashod ended his call.
"Girl, get over here and lay down."
"Oh, hell naw! Who the fuck was that?"
"That was just... don't worry about it. If it was something then I wouldn't have answered the phone with you sitting right here. I'm not stupid." Diamond thought about it and laid back down, but she wasn't stupid either and she was going to make sure he didn't go anywhere that night.

After the movie was over, Diamond suggested ice cream, from the local ice cream parlor. She got her boys together and they all went out. She tried to eat slow and kept trying to make conversation with Rashod, but it seemed as if his mind was somewhere else. When they got back home, around nine forty-five, Diamond figured she'd "give it to him" real good and he'd fall asleep, but it didn't work. Rashod helped her take the sleeping children into the house and put them to bed.
"Diamond, I'm about to step out for a minute, I'll call you later."
"Where are you going?," Diamond asked.
"Just to hang out for a minute." She walked up close to him and kissed him on the lips, he kissed her back, with only a peck so she moved even closer and kissed him again, this time

while trying to unbuckle his pants but Rashod pushed her hands away.
"I said, I'll be right back," Rashod said through his teeth.
"Make love to me first." He shook his head from side to side as he pushed his way past her.
"Don't wait up," Rashod said as he closed the door. Diamond could not believe that Rashod was treating her like this. It had to be another woman and she was going to find out who she was.

CHAPTER - 16

The next morning, Rashod walked into Diamond's house like nothing happened the night before. Diamond was disgusted with him but didn't show it; she had to be nice so that she could get the information that she needed.
"So, where have you been all night?," Diamond asked.
"I told you I was going to be spending more time with my mom's. Ever since I got out, I've basically been here. I haven't gotten to spend any time with my mom's in over eight years."
"Oh, that's cool. I'm not trying to move in on Mama Latifah. How is she doing anyway?"
"She's good. She asked about you and I told her I'd bring you and the boys over later this week."
"That'll be nice." Diamond knew this was all a cover up, but she was going to play his little game, for now. "Do you want some breakfast?"
"No, moms made us a big breakfast this morning." Diamond became angry but kept her composure because she knew that was a lie; that bitch had made him breakfast. He went into the living room, laid down on the couch and started flipping through the channels on the television.
"Diamond, can you bring me something to drink?," Rashod yelled from the living room.
"I'm busy," she yelled back. He'd been with his bitch all night and she was not about to cater to his ass. She fed her boys, got them dressed and when she came back downstairs, Rashod was asleep. She stood there and stared at him for a few seconds and damn was he fine! She wanted to just strip him naked but instead, she looked for his cell phone because she knew he was a hard sleeper, and he was snoring very loud. She first patted his pants pockets, but it wasn't in there, so she went to find his jacket which was hanging on the kitchen chair

and bingo! She went upstairs to the bathroom and locked the door. She read his text messages which wasn't about anything to make her mad, then she checked his voicemail, and it was Sonya.

"Hey Boo. I had a real nice time last night. It was just like old times. I can't wait to see you again. I love you." Diamond got so upset that her legs went limp. She held her breath so she wouldn't cry, and she counted backwards from ten like Dr. Floyd had instructed her when she became upset, then called Sonya. She went through Rashod's phone log, found her name and pressed talk. Sonya noticed her man's number and answered the phone.

"Hey Boo."

"This is not your Boo. This is Diamond, Rashod's woman. What do y'all call yourselves doing?"

"What do you mean, what do we think we're doing? Rashod and I have been together for eleven years. I held that brotha down when he was locked up. Shit, we go out of town every other weekend and we are about to make things back like they were before he went to jail."

"Well, ever since Rashod has been out, he's been here taking care of me and my boys, so you are old news. Now get used to it."

"Never old, only better. If you could let your imagination go for a minute and think about all the things Rashod and I did last night," she chuckled. "I'm not mad at you because obviously, you weren't aware, but I'm going to let you know woman to woman; don't put your heart into Rashod because he's coming home to mama." Diamond sat there quietly for a moment; she wasn't about to let this go down like this.

"Naw Boo, Rashod ain't going nowhere. He's happy with me and my boys and he wouldn't play me like that. If he fucked you last night than that's all you were, a fuck and now, he's back home to mommy."

"You' re a simple bitch, but I guess you'll learn." Diamond heard Rashod coming up the stairs.
"Diamond, who are you yelling at?"
"Look, I'm not your bitch," Diamond said lowering her voice, "and I'd appreciate it if you didn't call my man's phone anymore because you will get fucked up." Diamond glanced at Sonya's phone number and put it in her mental phone book, she hung up the phone, and put it in the dirty clothes hamper just as Rashod opened the bathroom door.
"Who are you yelling at?," he asked again.
"What are you talking about?," Diamond answered innocently. She grabbed his wife beater T-shirt, pulled him close to her and kissed his lips.
"Where were you all night?," Rashod stuck to his original story.
"At my mom's. Get dressed because she wants to see you and the boys." She closed the bathroom door and took off her clothes. He tried to ignore her while he brushed the waves in his hair. She sat on the bathroom sink opening her legs as wide as they could go.
"You turned this away last night for another bitch?" Rashod looked at her already wet vagina and became instantly turned on. Although he and Sonya had rough and freaky sex all night, today was a new day and he could go one more round. He put his lips between Diamond's legs and made her cum three times back-to-back. He pulled her off the sink and bent her over the toilet seat and beat it as hard as he could. Diamond had to grab the towel off the towel bar and smother her face to muffle her loud moaning because she didn't want to get the kid's attention. Rashod went to the shower and turned it on, guided Diamond into the shower without saying a word, got in with her and lifted her up wrapping her legs around his waist. He had her up against the shower wall making her almost want to cry, his loving was so good, but she just couldn't shake Sonya's voice from her head. She was

wondering if he had done the same thing to her last night. She put her legs on the floor of the tub.

"Hold up baby. Let me get my towel." She knew he wasn't done because he hadn't cum yet, so she grabbed her towel and wiped her face. He was still behind the shower curtain stroking his long manhood. Diamond opened the hamper, took out his cell phone and pressed the redial button and got back into the shower. She bent over letting the water run on her behind. Rashod came behind her and began making love to her slower. Diamond started moaning.

"Oh shit, Rashod. Do your pussy feel good to you?"

"Hell yeah!" he yelled back while he grabbed her waist and pounded as hard as he could. Their bodies were slapping together real hard, and Diamond moaned a little louder than usual, hoping that Sonya was still on the line.

"Oh baby, I'm cumin," yelled Rashod.

"Cum in your woman, baby," and Rashod did just that as he loudly moaned. Sonya had sat on the phone and listened to Diamond and Rashod make love. She started to cry, she knew she was dealing with a dirty bitch and had to find a way to get back at her. Diamond and Rashod finished their shower and got dressed. They went to Latifah's house, where she made them all corned beef sandwiches, soda and popcorn while they watched a movie. Diamond felt great because she knew Sonya had heard them and if she didn't, it was on her voicemail, and she would hear it soon. Hopefully, she would leave Rashod alone.

CHAPTER - 17

The next morning, Rashod went to Sonya's house, but his key didn't work. He thought something had to be wrong because he had called Sonya several times the night before but got no answer and now his key no longer worked. He began to beat on her door while Sonya sat on her bed and watched him from her surveillance camera. He kicked her door, banged on it as hard as he could as he called her name and tried his key once more before he left. Sonya ran downstairs, out the back door and got into her car, not the car like Rashod's but her 2005 black Chevy Impala because it would be less obvious. Sonya watched to see in which direction he was going before she pulled out of her driveway and followed him, trying to stay two cars behind. He got on the highway, which made it easier for her to keep up. He came to his exit and when he put on his blinker Sonya slowed down until he was off the ramp and watched which way he turned. She came around the corner just in time to see Rashod pull in a driveway. She sat at the corner and watched Rashod use his very own key to let himself in. She was devastated at this two timing bastard, but in reality, he hadn't committed himself to Sonya - people have to learn to understand that just because you're sleeping with a person and doing freaky things, that doesn't make him/her yours; make things clear before you go assuming - so Sonya sat there for almost an hour and cried, once she got herself together, she called his cell phone.
"Hey, you," Sonya said acting as if she wasn't upset.
"Where have you been? I just left the house, and my key didn't work. You didn't let me in, and I was about to kick that fuckin'' door in. You better be lucky I got some shit going for me right now."
"Oh well, I had to change the locks for a good reason, and I must have been in the shower or something when you came

by. So where are you right now?" Sonya was afraid to tell him the whole truth.

"Just out and about. Why? What's going on?"

"I wanted to see you real quick. We need to talk."

"Give me like an hour or so and then I'll call you." Sonya just hung up. She knew he was with that bitch and now she knew where "they" stayed. Now she had to think of a plan to get them both, Diamond for being a bitch and Rashod for trying to play her after she'd been there for him through the thick and thin. Basically, she had her life on hold for a dude that was locked up and she should be mad at herself, but she was going to make Rashod pay for misleading her.

Sonya sat at the corner for another twenty minutes trying to come up with something good, but she couldn't think of anything good enough so she just road past Diamond's house hoping to see what she looked like and why he would play her for Diamond, but she had no luck. She went home and cried again while Diamond and Rashod made love.

The next morning, Sonya got up early because she couldn't sleep, she took Jeff to Latifah's, just in case they decided to go there. She went back to Diamond's house and parked up the street where she could see her house. She sat there for four hours before she seen some movement. Diamond opened the door, came outside to get her mail and was carrying a newborn baby. Sonya automatically assumed it was Rashod's, she got out of her car and ran down the street. Diamond saw her coming, but she didn't know her, so she assumed she was just running down the street until she stopped in front of Diamond's steps.

"Are you Diamond?," Sonya asked.

"Who's asking?," Diamond said, and Sonya recognized her voice.

"Uh, yeah. You're that bitch."

"Who the fuck are you calling a bitch? You don't even know me."

"Is that Rashod's baby you got?"

"Na..." Diamond didn't finish her answer. "Why? How do you know Rashod, or even where I stay?"

"You haven't figured it out yet, huh? Rashod is my man. You see that Cadi up there? Yes, we have his and her cars. Do you see this ring on my finger? Yes, he bought it."

"Well, you're the dummy because he's here with me almost every night and has been ever since he came home. Stay right there, I'll go get Rashod and he can let us both know what's up." Diamond went into the house and put Deontae' down, went upstairs and woke up Rashod.

"You need to get dressed and come downstairs. There's some bitch at the door talking about she's your fiancé' and that y'all got matching Cadillacs and everything else."

"Yeah right. Man, gone with that bullshit."

"I'm serious. Now get up."

"Then why are you so calm about it?"

"Because I don't believe her, and I want you to come down here and prove me right." Rashod knew it had to be Sonya, but how did she know where he was? He was on another side of town, and no one knew him over there. He slowly put on his black Sean John jogging pants thinking of a good line to give them both to keep himself safe because they both were bat shit crazy. He put on his white Sean John t-shirt and white Nike tennis shoes and went downstairs. When he got to the door, no one was there.

"Why do you play so much?"

"It was someone here. She had a maroon Cadillac with a big tire on the back just like yours, she was a little bit shorter than me, had a long burgundy weave, brown skinned and she wasn't all that cute, if you ask me."

"First of all, I didn't ask you. I don't know nobody that looks like that or wears a weave."

"You know what, I'll call that bitch, because we are going to get to the bottom of this today." Rashod started to laugh as he sat on the couch. He wanted to see her call Sonya because his cell phone was in his pocket, and he just knew that she didn't have her number. Diamond went upstairs and got her cell phone, dialed Sonya's number and put her phone on speaker.

"Hello, Sonya. This is Diamond. Why did you leave? Were you afraid of the truth?" Rashod sat up on the couch with his eyes open wide; he was in shock.

"What are you talking about? Who is Diamond?" Sonya knew she was on speaker and that Rashod was listening and she was not going to give him that satisfaction. She knew that he would kill her if he knew that she had been to his other woman's house, they had been through this before.

"Don't play stupid. You were at my house a couple of minutes ago because I went outside to get my mail and you came running down the street."

"You are crazy. I don't know you and why in the hell would I be running down your street? I don't even know where you live." Diamond had to think for a minute, was she tripping?

"*Naw, I'm not crazy,*" Diamond said to herself.

"You were just here, and I have Rashod here so now, we can get to the bottom of this."

"Oh, Rashod had you call me?" Sonya knew she had her losing her mind and Rashod was going to think that she was either crazy or a liar. That was a start for her.

"No, I called you on my own."

"Is Rashod there with you? Tell him I said hello and that I'll call him because I have to go, I have things to do," Sonya hung up the phone.

"Why are you playing games? If you wanted to ask me about her, you should've just asked. Rashod got up off the couch.

"I'm about to go. I have some thinking to do. Man, I don't know about you. You be on some silly, childish ass shit and I don't have time for that. You're starting unnecessary drama."

"Come on Rashod, let's use our common sense. How would I know who she is if she wasn't just here?"
"Who knows. You got her number? You probably went over her house." Rashod got his black Sean John jacket and left thinking that Diamond had something to do with Sonya changing her locks. He wanted so badly to go to Sonya's house, but he had to figure out what was going on first, so he went to his mom's where he knew he would be safe.

CHAPTER - 18

Several weeks had passed and Sonya was completely ignoring Rashod Diamond was still around, but she wasn't in love with him like she used to be, even though they were still together.

Diamond had started noticing a big change in Rashod, not only was he not staying at her place, but his appearance changed and so did his sex drive, a lot of times he couldn't even get it up, he was constantly smoking marijuana and every time he went to the bathroom he had to lock the door. She was totally distraught. She assumed it was the other woman, Sonya, but she'd check his phone log, texts, and voicemail and it didn't seem like they'd been spending that much time together, either. She would listen at the bathroom door and all she could hear was water running. One afternoon, Rashod and some of his boys were doing their usual, sitting around playing spades, smoking and drinking, and this time they invited Diamond. She joined in and smoked a blunt with them and became extremely high, so high that she had to go to bed. She assumed it was because she hadn't really been kicking it since she had Deontae'. Later that night before they went to bed, Rashod offered her another blunt.

"Here baby, smoke this with me. I know I haven't been putting it down like I used to, but I've had a lot on my mind. Let's get blowed out of our minds and sex all night." She was with that! Diamond smoked the already rolled blunt that Rashod had in his shirt pocket. It not only made her sleepy, but it also made her see black spots all over her hands, but she felt great, and had a high that she didn't want to come off.

"Baby, what kind of weed is this? I've been smoking for a while and I've never been this high," Diamond said.

"Just enjoy it baby because I've got plenty of blow."

"What's blow?," Diamond asked.
"Oh, it's just some bomb ass shit," Rashod said while laughing. Diamond did everything that Rashod told her to do that night and didn't remember half of it the next morning, but she knew that she wanted another blunt.

A week had passed, Diamond and Rashod were high almost every day. She hadn't gotten her kids dressed and they were eating junk food or cereal all day and she was half eating herself and began to lose a lot of weight. When Diamond saw Rosetta the first thing she asked her, was she sick?
"Diamond baby, what's wrong with you? You look all sick, your hair is a mess and look at my grandsons. They look like they haven't had a bath in a week and look at their hair. When was the last time they had a haircut?"
"Mom, I've been a little under the weather, but I'm better now." Rosetta knew better, she knew something was going on in her daughter's life. Her house looked like holy hell and so did she.
"Diamond, let's go to lunch, Nikki and I will straighten up a little while you get dressed and get the boys together." Rosetta cleaned all the trash off the table, swept the floor, and moved the couch so that she could run the sweeper. She almost had a heart attack. She found a mirror, a razor blade, two bags of cocaine, some pills, a bag of marijuana and two hundred dollars. She gathered it up and put it into a baggy and into her purse. Now, she knew what her daughter's problem was, she was hooked on drugs, and she had to figure out a way to get her some help.

Rosetta took Diamond and her kids to Ann's Steak and Crab House, Diamond's favorite restaurant, hoping to get her to talk. It was a Wednesday afternoon, and she knew it wouldn't be crowded. Diamond ordered Alaskan King crab legs, baked potato with sour cream and butter and a house salad. Rosetta ordered a full slab of baby back ribs with an order of fries that she shared with her grandkids. Diamond ate everything on her plate. She hadn't had a good meal in at least a week.

"So, Diamond, what's going on in your life?" Rosetta asked.

"What do you mean?" Rosetta wanted to tell her about the drugs she found, but she didn't want her to try to lie and she didn't want her grandchildren to know what was going on.

"I don't know, you've just changed, I've never seen your house look like that and you think that you're fine as wine and you look a mess." They both laughed. "I know you're not letting that sorry man that's been staying over there turn you out. Every time I call, the kids say that you're in bed or on the couch sleep. Are you bored? Do you need some way to occupy your time?"

"Mom, I've told you that I've been a little under the weather, but I'm alright now. I was planning on cleaning up my house this weekend. I wasn't expecting any company."

"How about you and the boys stay the rest of the week with me?"

"Why?"

"Just so we can spend some overdue time together."

"I guess. Let me go home and get some clothes." Diamond went home and got all her dirty laundry, so she could wash over her mothers and an outfit for her and the boys. Rosetta knew she wasn't going to let her go home for a couple of days and was going to find a way to make them stay.

Friday morning, Diamond got up and was ready to go home; she missed her man and she wanted another "blunt".

"Alright mom, the boys and I are going home today. I enjoyed spending time with you, but I want to go home."

"We are going to go and register Brandon for preschool. He should've been in there several months ago. Have you even been reading to him?" Diamond didn't answer. "You stay here and get dressed. I'll be back in about a half an hour, so be ready." Rosetta went to Diamond's apartment to look around, she had Diamond's keys, so she let herself in and the smoke greeted her at the door, and she saw Rashod and his boys' doing lines of cocaine.

"What the hell? You know what, the party's over, you crackheads got to go!"

"This is not your house. You are not about to come down here trying to run no show! Where is Diamond anyway?" Rashod asked while wiping his nose and trying to hide the evidence. Rashod hadn't really spoken to Diamond since he had left Wednesday morning, she had called him once and they were able to talk for a few seconds, because Rosetta stayed up under her all day and when she left, she would take the phone off the hook in her bedroom and lock her door. Diamond had forgotten her phone charger at home and the battery was dead, so she had no way of using the phone. Rashod didn't have her mother's phone number and even if he did, he probably wouldn't call her house because he was not one of her favorite people and she made sure that he knew it, too.

"This is not your house either and I would advise you to leave before I call the police. I know that you're on probation and you shouldn't be smoking weed or smoking crack or whatever the hell you're doing." Rashod became instantly pissed because he assumed that Diamond had sent her mother to do her dirty work, by putting them out. He got up and gathered all his drugs and they were about to leave.

"Oh, hell no! You better get in there and clean up that mess before you leave, this house was clean the last time I was here and Diamond and the boys haven't been here, so I know that you and your cracked ass friends are the ones that messed it up." Rashod and his boys got up and cleaned up their mess with an attitude because they knew that Rosetta would call the police if they disrespected her or didn't do as they were told. As soon as they left, Rosetta called the building maintenance and told them that Diamond had lost her keys and needed the locks changed. She was informed that it would cost twenty-five dollars and they wouldn't be able to make it to her apartment until the next afternoon. Rosetta was fine with that and wasn't letting Diamond go home until it was done.

When Rosetta returned home, Diamond and the boys were dressed and ready to go. She had all of her dirty clothes washed, packed in two trash bags and waiting by the door and they were sitting in the living room watching television.
"Mom, we're ready when you are."
"Well, I'm not ready yet. Go in there and feed them boys some lunch and then put them down for a nap." Rosetta went upstairs to her bedroom. Diamond got up with an attitude and went and made her children grilled cheese sandwiches and French fries, she laid them down after they ate, and she and Rosetta watched some movies. In the meantime, Rashod was thinking "*forget Diamond,*" and he was going to get all his things out of her house. He went inside and looked under the couch to get his packages because he had to get himself right before he started packing and everything was gone. He turned the couch upside down and still found nothing. Rashod was pissed. The only thing that he could think of was Diamond had gotten him; she had taken all his drugs, money and had left. He thought that he had really turned her into a crackhead, but she knew nothing about his drugs or money. Rashod went ballistic, he went upstairs, started going through Diamond's drawers and throwing everything onto the floor and even ransacked her closet, but he found nothing. He laid back on the bed to gather his thoughts; he tried calling her cell phone, but it went straight to voicemail, so he left her a message.
"Oh bitch, you want to try to fuckin" play me? Wait until I see you! I knew I shouldn't have given you no coke! You're acting like a fucking crackhead already, but I got something for yo ass and all of my shit better turn up!," He hung up, went downstairs, got a pair of scissors and returned to Diamond's

bedroom; he cut all of her bras in half, all the toes out of her socks and the crouch out of her panties, all while he was waiting for her to return his call. He picked up his phone and called her again but again, it went straight to voicemail. He went to her closet and started on her clothes, he ripped the buttons off her shirts, cut up her timberland boots, broke the heels off of her high heel sandals, cut the legs off a couple pair of her pants and then took a nap. When he woke up, he could vaguely remember what had happened. He got up, went to Sonya's house to try to make things up with her because he knew that once Diamond seen her place, she wasn't going to have anything else to do with him.

The next morning, Diamond listened to her voicemail and was wondering what the hell Rashod was talking about? She understood now why she was so high and needed Rashod's blunts, as well as, had the urge to stay high all day. She was pissed, not only at him but at herself for not knowing. She realized why Rosetta was keeping her hostage. Everything was finally coming together, but she couldn't figure out how her mother knew what was going on. Diamond got up and took a long, hot shower to try to get her head right. She got dressed and decided to get out of the house for a little while because she had some business she needed to take care of.

"Mom, can you watch the boys for a minute while I walk to the store to get a pack of cigarettes? I need some fresh air." Rosetta agreed, because the store wasn't that far and she knew that her cell phone wasn't working, so she figured she couldn't call anyone. She lived too far to walk home, and she probably did need a breath of fresh air. When Diamond got to the store, the first thing she did was took seventy-five cents and called Rashod from the pay phone. He answered on the second ring.

"Hello?"

"What's up with that message you left me last night?," Diamond asked.
"Where are you?"
"At the pay phone outside of the store by my mother's house."
"Stay there, I'm coming to get you." Diamond went inside the store, bought a pack of Basic cigarettes and waited outside by the pay phone for Rashod to pick her up. When he arrived, she jumped in the Cadi, and he just started driving.
"Where are we going?"
"Just sit back and enjoy the ride. So did you miss me?"
"I need to go home and get my phone charge. I did miss you until I got your message last night. So, you're telling me that you were trying to turn me out like that?," Diamond began to cry. "You know that I'm raising my boys all by myself. I trusted you to be in my corner to help me, not to bring me down."
"Well, you don't need your phone charger right now." He didn't want her to see what he had done to her house, so he wasn't going that way. "Let's go to my mom's house for a minute." He knew that Latifah was at church and wouldn't be home for at least three to four hours, so they would have the house all to themselves. When they got in the house, he locked all the doors, he even put the chains on them so no one would walk in on them. Rashod treated Diamond like the ho that she was, by making her take off all her clothes and he used her socks to tie her hands to the headboard. He stuck his manhood in her mouth and tried to shove it down her throat and she was beginning to choke, but she couldn't push him away because he had tied her up pretty good, so she bit him. He smacked her across the face.
"Rashod, I don't know what the fuck your problem is, but you need to let me loose and take me home, because I'm not feeling this."
"Bitch, you stole from me! That was almost five hundred dollars' worth of my shit that you took."

"What the fuck are you talking about? I didn't take nothing from you!" Rashod didn't want to hear nothing she had to say, he put her legs over her shoulders and entered her from behind.
"Rashod! I just told you I don't want to do this, this is rape!" He ignored her and sexed her as hard as he could, and Diamond started to cry.
"Rashod that hurts!"
"Shut up bitch! You want to play rough, then take it rough." He pulled his penis out and put a condom on and entered her vagina. He gently kissed her tears away and untied her hands. Rashod still loved Diamond, but he felt betrayed, and the drugs were making him a different person. He made love to her so good that when they were done, she had forgotten that he had tried to choke her with his penis and that he tried to tear her a new butthole. They laid there and smoked what Diamond was now aware of, a primo and she had been craving it for the past three days. They took a long, hot bath just in case Diamond tried to go to the police and say that he raped her; there wouldn't be any evidence. Rashod burned a vanilla incense, changed the linen and put the dirty sheets in the washer. They got dressed and left Latifah's house before she returned from church.

Rashod took Diamond to the woods so they could be alone, because they needed to talk.
"Why are we here? Rashod I need to get back home because my mother is probably worrying about me," Diamond said, and she was right. Rosetta had put Diamond's boys in the car and was riding around looking for her. She went to the corner store and was told that she had been there like an hour ago, and had bought some cigarettes, but they didn't see her after she left the store. Rosetta knew that she was with Rashod but didn't know where he lived or even his last name. She went to Diamond's house thinking maybe they were there but when

she went inside and saw Diamond's torn up house, she instantly knew that her daughter was in danger. She told the kids to stay in the car while she called the police and searched the house, hoping that she didn't find her daughter's body in there and luckily she didn't. What she did find was all of Diamond's clothes cut up and her bedroom disorganized. When the police arrived, they took a report and Rosetta told them that Rashod was probably the one who did all of this because she had put him and his friends out earlier, but they couldn't do anything because no one seen him do it. They just said it was vandalism, the landlord came out and changed her locks for free. Rosetta also informed the police that her daughter was missing, and she thought that she was in danger, but the police said that she had to be missing for at least twenty-four hours because she was an adult and that she was probably where she wanted to be, but they would investigate it for her. Rosetta was right; Diamond was in trouble.

"Don't play stupid! You know why we're here. Where is my money and the rest of my shit?," Rashod asked.

"I told you that I don't know what you're talking about."

"I had two hundred dollars, some weed, some pills and some cocaine under the couch in the living room and it's all gone."

"Well, I didn't take it! Why in the hell would you have that shit where my kids can reach it?"

"I was getting my shit together and you came downstairs, so I just threw it under the couch real quick so you wouldn't be all in my mix. The kids were sleep and I planned on taking it with me the next morning, but I forgot and when I came back to get my shit after your mother put me out, it was gone!" Diamond sat there thinking.

"I know exactly which day you're talking about because I saw you push something under the couch and..." Rashod cut her off and pulled out his Smith & Wesson.

"So, now you're admitting that you took my shit?" Diamond lost her whole train of thought.

"What are you doing with that gun?"
"Where is my shit?" Diamond started to cry.
"My mother and my daughter had cleaned up my downstairs while I got the boys dressed and she must have taken it. That's probably why she won't let me go home."
"You are so juvenile. You need to grow the fuck up and keep your mommy out of your business! So how am I supposed to get my shit back?" He put the Smith & Wesson to her head.
"I will get it baby, I promise and if I can't, when I get my check I'll pay you myself if I have to. How much was it?"
"It was about five hundred dollars' worth of shit, but I need commission, so I need at least seven."
"Why are you trying to play me? You told me that you loved me and my boys and you're going to let some money come between us?" He looked at her and started to laugh. "What's so funny?"
"The thought of shooting you is making my dick hard."
Diamond had to think fast, she knew now that she was dealing with a sick bastard. He had gone to jail for attempted murder once and this time, it may not be attempted because he might kill her.
"Well, you know that the store has cameras and I'm sure that someone saw me get into your car. My mother'll be looking for me."
"You know what? At this point, I really don't give a damn. My woman has betrayed me, Sonya don't fuck with me anymore because of you, my mother has been acting funny the last couple of days, so I really don't have anywhere to go. At least, if I go back to jail, I'll get three good meals a day, a place to lay my head at night, a nice gym to workout in and I won't have to deal with all this drama that I'm dealing with now."
"Rashod, you have come a long way. You got out of jail, have a couple of trades, you're very smart, all you need to do is apply yourself. I heard you and your boys talking and you

have a good job lined up; all you have to do is get off all these drugs and get yourself together. You will do well." Rashod sat down on a rock, put his hand over his face, put his gun on his lap and started to think.

"Diamond, you're a good woman and I don't want to lose you. I am just so confused right now. If it weren't for you, I don't know what I'd be doing right now."

"We will always be friends." Diamond walked over to Rashod to give him a hug and when he hugged her back, she took his Smith & Wesson and threw it as hard as she could.

"Why the fuck did you do that shit? I need that." He got up to see if he could find his Smith & Wesson and she took off running the opposite way. He started to chase her, but he changed his mind. He had to find his Smith & Wesson because it had his fingerprints on it and he needed some protection because he had been doing some stupid stuff the past couple of weeks. He searched the area for almost an hour before he found his Smith & Wesson and by that time, Diamond had gone to a nearby store and called Rosetta, but she wasn't at home. She was still looking for her daughter. Diamond called a taxi and went back to her mother's house where she knew she would be safe. She and Rosetta pulled up at the same time. Diamond had never been so happy to see her. She ran to her as fast as she could and they embraced, she didn't even pay the cab driver.

"Hey, get back here!," the taxi driver yelled as he jumped out of the taxi to chase Diamond but when he saw that she was just greeting her mother, he stood there and waited patiently, he had noticed her crying in the back seat of the taxi, but he had learned to mind his own business, so he never asked her why she was crying. Rosetta went and paid the taxi driver, although Diamond had her own money, she was showing her daughter that she cared and that if she needed her, she was there.

CHAPTER - 19

Rosetta had contacted Diamond's father, James when she found the drugs in her daughter's house hoping that she could get a change of environment. James informed her that she was welcome to come anytime but he only had a one-bedroom apartment, so it wasn't enough room for her and her kids but if he had to, he would give them his bedroom and they could make pallets on the floor, but Rosetta was willing to keep her grandkids so that Diamond could get her life together.

"Diamond, how do you feel about going to stay with your father in Columbus, Ohio for a couple of months? Or just until you get yourself together."

"You mean my dad because I don't have a father. I've only seen that man once or twice in my adult life and he don't give a fu... care about me or he would've tried to be in me and my kid's life. He calls me every now and then, but he don't do nothing for me."

"He cares, it was me. He wasn't there for me like I wanted him to be, so I wouldn't allow him to be in your life, but I have prayed about a lot of things. I have been going to church for the right reasons and I think that I am a new woman. I want everything to be right for my family. Diamond, I don't know what's going on in your life, but I want things to be better for you. I know that I always have something to say about your boyfriends, but I actually like Vonte'. He made some bad choices, but I honestly believe that he was doing it for you and the boys. Now, this new dude that you got; you need to let him go back where he came from." Diamond knew that Rosetta was right, but she never admitted it. "Diamond, I found all these drugs and money in your house. Was it yours?" Diamond shook her head.

"No, but did you take it?"

"Yes, I did. I didn't know if it was yours or not and I didn't want my grandkids to accidentally get a hold of it and eat it or something."

"Well, Mom, Rashod tried to kill me because of that, and he raped me." Diamond began to cry. "He took me into the woods, and I actually thought that I was dead, but I think that an angel was watching over me." Rosetta held her daughter and they cried together.

"Baby, promise me that you will leave Rashod, because I would hate to have to go to jail for this fool doing something to you or my grandkids."

"Mom, I promise."

"So, will you go and stay with your father for a couple of months?" Diamond gave Rosetta a funny look with a half-smile.

"No, I would like to get to know him a little better first. He could be some sick pervert." They both began to laugh.

"I understand but I don't want Rashod to hurt you."

"I'll be alright. He has shown me a side that I don't want to see again." They hugged and Rosetta went to get the fried chicken, macaroni and cheese, collard greens and cornbread finished up for dinner that she had started, and Diamond went looking for Rashod's drugs and money. She had Brandon sit outside Rosetta's door and told him to start coughing when he saw Nikki or his grandmother. She searched her room, went through her closet, looked under her bed and in her drawers and bingo! She found the baggy with the pills, marijuana, cocaine, money and small mirror she put it down her pants. They ate dinner and Diamond asked Rosetta to take them home.

Diamond entered her house, and her legs went limp. She almost fell to the ground, Rosetta had forgotten to warn her about her disastrous house; the couch was flipped over, all the glasses and plates were thrown out of the cabinet.

Diamond reached for her cell phone to call the police and Rosetta grabbed it out of her hand.

"I already called them, baby and there is nothing that they can do because no one saw what happened." Diamond went to the neighbors and was told that no one saw anything. Rosetta helped her clean up the mess, but the kids continued to get in the way.

"Mom, I can clean this up myself. I need some time to think anyway, so can you just keep the boys for the night?"

"Anything baby. Oh, I had the locks changed so that nothing ass nigga can't get in your house. If he comes by here then call the police, don't even fool with him." Rosetta handed Diamond a copy of her new keys and gave her cell phone back.

"I will Mom because he's going to pay for this." Diamond finished cleaning up the downstairs and headed upstairs. When she saw her clothes all cut up, she sat down on the bed and started to cry. She took the baggy out of her pants, did two lines of cocaine, smoked her a blunt and went to sleep.

The next morning, Diamond got up and threw everything in the trash, all her good clothes and shoes were gone to waste. She called Rashod, who had made amends with Sonya and when he saw her name come up on his phone, he pressed ignore so she left him a voicemail.

"You sick bastard! You want to cut up my shit? I got something for you! I got your little two hundred dollars, but I'm going to use that to replace as much of my shit as I can. I'm going to smoke the rest of this weed and cocaine and I'm going to sell the rest of this shit. If you bring your punk ass around here, I'm going to have somebody fuck you up, better yet, I'm going to call the police so they can put your sick ass back in jail." Diamond was so pissed that she smoked the rest of Rashod's weed lacing it with the cocaine. She knew that it would piss Rashod off, so she called Sonya's phone.

"Sonya, this is Diamond. I'm quite sure you know my voice by now."

"Why are you calling my phone? Rashod didn't answer his so that means that he don't want to talk to you."

"Oh, so he's back with you, huh?"

"I told you he wasn't going anywhere, what you thought?"

"He's only there because I don't want him anymore."

"Then why are you calling around looking for him?"

"He owes me some money for tearing up my shit. The little money that he left here is not enough."

"If he pays you, will you leave us the hell alone?"

"I sure will. I need at least four hundred dollars."

"For what?"

"He cut up all of my clothes and my boots." Sonya began to chuckle.

"Oh, he got you, too? I'll give you two and that's it."

"I see why he stays with you. You are a stupid bitch."

"Naw, I just know how to keep my man."

"By paying off his debts, letting him go out and have his fun and then, come back to you? You don't know what he's picking up out there, because he don't use a rubber. The first time we had sex, it was bare-back, and he didn't even know anything about me."

"Well, that makes you a nasty ho."

"That's alright because that makes you nasty, too because you're fucking right after me. Boy, I sure hope that Rashod don't give you something that you can't get rid of."

"What are you trying to say?" Diamond started to laugh.

"You better go and get your shit checked."

"Bitch I will..." Diamond hung up the phone.

By the end of the week, all of Rashod's drugs were gone. Diamond sold the pills to one of her neighbors and went to a closeout store and replaced all her dishes for twenty dollars. She took the rest of the money and bought herself some more clothes and drugs. She couldn't replace everything, but she did alright.

Diamond decided to leave Rashod alone because he is who he is and nothing was going to change, but she needed him and his drugs. He knew that she would soon look for him to return. Diamond called Rashod three to four times a day and he never answered.

One night, Diamond was sitting outside on her stoop and saw Rashod's Cadi pull around the corner from her house. She didn't know whether to get up and run in the house or call the police and hide. Her neighbors were outside, and kids were playing basketball in the street, so if he did anything to her, there would be witnesses. She continued to sit on the stoop. At first, Rashod just rode past and twenty minutes later, he pulled in her driveway. She didn't move, she just stared at him. He got out of the car looking better than he did the first day that they met; his blue Prada shorts were neatly pressed like they had just come out of the cleaners, a short sleeve striped Prada shirt that was buttoned half- way showing his hairy, buff chest and brand-new blue and white Lebron tennis shoes and she could smell his cologne as soon as he stepped out of the car. Rashod walked up on the steps like they had talked yesterday.

"What's up babe?," Rashod asked.

"Nothing. Where have you been the last two weeks? I haven't heard from you."

"Just getting my head together. I almost lost my cool over you and I'm trying to be a better person." Diamond was a sucker for lines and could never tell when a guy was running game on her.

"Yeah, you're right. Where are the boys?"

"That's what love and some good ass does to you." Rashod started laughing.

"Deontae's in the house sleep and the other two are at daycare."

"So that means we have time to make up for missed time?"

"No, I'm not in the mood for that."

"Why? You found another man? If you did, you might as well call and cancel that right now, because I'm back."

"No, I'm not looking for anyone. It's too many 'crazy' people out here." Diamond looked at Rashod, referring to him. He knew what she was saying but ignored her statement.

"Come on, let's go in the house and chill for a minute. I just ran into my dude who claims he has some real fire." Diamond was on that; she hadn't had a good blunt in a couple of days. Rashod handed her two hundred dollars then they got up and went into the house.

"Sorry about all your shit. I don't know what got into me that night." They sat down and started playing a game of dominoes and Rashod took an already rolled blunt out of his pocket, lit it up and they smoked the whole thing. Everything that Rashod said to her after that sounded like it was in slow motion, he looked blurry, she kept seeing black spots and her face felt numb. Rashod went to his car; got the bottle of Patron he had been drinking and they finished the bottle. Diamond laid on the couch and fell asleep, she was awakened by a loud pounding at her door, she rolled over, looked at the clock and it read 5:45 PM.

"Aww fuck!" Diamond yelled as she jumped up from the couch, she had forgot to pick up the boys from daycare and they had called Rosetta.

"So, you're starting this dumb shit again?" Diamond looked in the driveway and Rashod's car was gone, so she could come up with a lie.

"Oh my gosh Mom, I was watching TV and I must've dozed off. They didn't try to call my cell phone."

"They said they tried to call the house phone and your cell phone several times and I called it myself."

"Oh well, I let the house phone get shut off, because I have a cell phone. That's just an extra bill that I don't need." Diamond looked at her cell phone and had six missed calls.
"Man, I must've been sleeping pretty hard because I didn't even hear my cell phone ring." Diamond had a splitting headache, and her eyes were bloodshot red.
"What the hell is wrong with your eyes?"
"I have a headache, that's why I was sleep. I took four extra strength pain pills." Diamond was lying.
"Why did you take so many?"
"Because my headache wouldn't go away after I took two, so I took two more and they must've made me fall asleep."
Rosetta wanted to believe her, but she didn't.
"Alright. Do you need me to keep the boys for the night?"
"Could you please?," Diamond asked.
"I'll keep the two youngest, but Brandon can stay here, just in case, he needs to call 9-1-1." Rosetta knew that she would see Brandon the next day and he would fill her in on everything that Diamond was doing. Diamond was cool with Brandon staying because she could make him go to bed early and he could pretty much watch himself. When Rosetta left, Diamond went inside and made her son a Daffy Duck spaghetti and meatball, corn and oatmeal cookie microwave dinner, put him in front of the cartoons, went outside and called Rashod.
"What happened to you earlier?"
"I had some runs to make, and you were sleep. I didn't want to wake you."
"Well, I needed to get my kids and they called my mother. You know they will take my kids for that shit."
"My bad baby. Next time, I'll wake you up." Diamond felt in her bra and the two hundred dollars wasn't there. She went into the house as she continued to talk on the phone and looked through the couch.
"Rashod, do you remember where I put that money?"
"Yeah, you put it in your shirt or something."

"That's funny, I can't find it."
"Well, I gave it to you." While Diamond was sleep, Rashod took his money back.

One night, Diamond and Rashod were sitting back smoking a primo, drinking a bottle of vodka, and just talking. Rashod stopped and began to stare at her.
"What?," asked Diamond.
"Diamond, I've been thinking, we've been together for a while. I know we've been through a lot of bullshit, but I want to make things right with us." She was shocked, but she knew that Rashod was going to ask her to marry him.
"Oh, yeah?," she said with a smile on her face.
"Yeah. Why don't you go out and uh..." He stopped and took a puff of his blunt. Her heart was beating five times faster than normal, like she had ran a marathon.
"And what?," Diamond asked.
"Uh, get a girl to join us in the bedroom."
"WHAT?" She yelled as she sat up closer to the table; Rashod had blown her high.
"Are you out of your damn mind? Do I look like a fuckin' lesbian to you? Let me go out and find a dude to join us in the bedroom."
"Oh, you want somebody to run a train on you. Now, that's nasty" Rashod said.
"That's not what I meant."
"Well, that's what you said." He was trying to turn things around to make her think that she was the one tripping. "Why are you so upset anyway? I'm doing this for us. I'm trying to make you happy and keep you satisfied. Don't tell me that you've never been with a chick?"
"No, and I'm not interested, either."
"Look, you know what you like, right?"
"What do you mean?," she asked.
"You know what it takes to keep you coming?"

"Yeah, and you're doing a fine job."
"Well baby, I just want to add some more excitement to our relationship. You can pick the girl, so I won't have any feelings for her." Diamond sat there and thought about it for a minute; she loved Rashod and would do anything for him, but this was a little out of her league, no one had ever asked her to do this before. Rashod saw her thinking about it, so he moved closer to her, kissed her on the lips, pulled the chair from the table and pulled up her skirt. He saw that she wasn't wearing any panties and he took advantage of the opportunity by kissing her thighs and her wet spot.
"So, are you thinking about it?"
"I don't know, Rashod."
"Come on, Diamond. Girl, you know I love you and I wouldn't do anything to hurt you. I'm just trying to make you happy." She sat there and enjoyed her moment with Rashod. Just when she was about to climax, Rashod got up.
"Baby, what are you doing? Come on, don't stop." Diamond pleaded as she squirmed out of control on the chair she was sitting in and trying to pull Rashod to her.
"Go find that chick and she'll give it to you like you want it." Rashod got up. Diamond pleased herself, but it wasn't as good as Rashod would have done it, so she thought about it and maybe Rashod was right.

The next day, Diamond went to The Hot Spot, a local night club, looking for her and her man a playmate.

CHAPTER - 20

Saturday night, Diamond put on a new outfit that she had bought when she got her check: a turquoise and white Roca wear drop waist dress, white Roca wear Rivera tote with an Amber rainbow Roca wear buckle-up wallet and white Roca wear strap up sandals with a two-inch heel that showed off her French manicured toes that she had done herself. Diamond had a lot of skills; she just didn't use them in all the right ways. She sat at the bar of the Hot Spot watching everyone and she was so confused. She saw a couple of girls that she thought was pretty, but she didn't know how to approach them, and she didn't want anybody that looked better than she did, so Diamond got up and went into the bathroom, went into a stall, took her wallet out of her purse and pulled a folded up one-dollar bill and snorted some cocaine. She felt great, wiped off her nose went and stood next to the DJ booth and watched the ladies line dance and she found that girl. Diamond watched the way she smiled, the way she moved her hips and the way she bit her bottom lip as she danced to the music.

Diamond knew all the line dances, so she decided to join in. She made her way next to the girl, hoping to make her their playmate.

"Hey, this dance is so cute. I've been trying to do it, but I can't get it," Diamond lied.

"Just follow my lead and I'll help you," the girl said.

Diamond played around acting like she couldn't get it and suddenly before the song ended; she caught on.

"Thanks, I think I can do it by myself now. What's your name?"

"Cassandra but everybody calls me CeCe."

"Alright CeCe. Can I buy you a drink to show my appreciation?"

"For what?," she asked, and she had the most beautiful smile.
"Showing me that dance. I've been trying to learn it for weeks."
"No, you don't have to do that."
"I insist."
"Alright, get me one of those bubble gum vodka drinks."
CeCe followed Diamond to the bar, and they were able to get two seats because the DJ was hot as always, and everyone was on the dance floor. Diamond wasn't sure as to how to get personal with CeCe without being too nosey and pushy.
"So, do you come here often?," Diamond asked.
"No, I work two jobs and I have a three-month-old son, so I don't get out too much but when I do, I try to party like a rock star." CeCe said as she threw her hands in the air.
"I know that's right. I have three boys and a girl, so I don't get out too much, either. So, what do you like to do for fun?"
"I don't know, play cards or dominoes and have a few drinks."
"Just my kind of girl," Diamond said and winked her eye at CeCe. "Let's exchange numbers and maybe we can hang out sometimes."
"I told you I don't get out too often because my job is demanding, and I don't really hang with nobody. I like to go out by myself," CeCe said.
"Oh, so you're here alone?"
"Oh! This is my song. It was really nice talking to you girl. Oh, and thanks for the drink." CeCe got up from the bar and made her way to the dance floor, ignoring Diamond's question. Diamond knew that she wasn't going to get her to do it and she didn't know how to approach a female because she didn't know who was straight or gay. She didn't want to approach any of the butch girls, where you can't tell if they're chicks or dudes, so she gave up and went home.

Diamond walked in the house looking as if she lost her best friend. Rashod was lying on the couch watching television with her boys. "So, how did it go tonight?"
"Man, I can't do this. I don't know which females to approach. I thought I had one, but she just brushed me off."
"Man, you can't do shit. You need me to hold your hand for everything. I'll ask my mom to babysit, and we'll go out together." He called Latifah and of course, she agreed to watch the boys for her son. They dropped the sleeping boys off and they headed to the Tina Cortez strip club. They pulled in the parking lot, sat in the car, smoked a blunt and did a line of cocaine. "Are you ready?," Rashod asked.
"As ready as I'm ever going to be." When they first entered the club, Diamond felt uncomfortable because all the girls were walking around totally naked like it was no big deal, but after a few drinks, she was smacking girls on their butts when they walked by. Diamond and Rashod watched a couple of the girls' dance, do splits and tricks on the pole. Rashod had spotted the girl that he wanted when he walked in the door and was hoping that Diamond picked the same girl.
"So, do you see anything that you like?," Rashod asked.
"Yeah, these girls are amazing. I can do this and make some good money."
"You're right, we'll hook that up later. Let's do what we came here for first." Diamond looked around until she found the perfect girl.
"How about her?," Diamond asked pointing to one of the girls.
"What about that girl over there?," Rashod asked pointing to the one he had seen earlier.
"She's alright. Why? Is that who you want?"
"It's your call, Boo," Rashod said smiling because he knew if he said yes then she wouldn't choose her.
"OK, then her," Diamond said choosing Rashod's choice.
"Hey, lovely lady," Rashod called to the stripper. "Bring that fat ass over here." Diamond smacked her lips and folded her

arms across her chest with attitude as the girl approached them.

"What's up, daddy?" The stripper wasn't as cute when she got closer, she was fair skinned, but she looked tired as if she'd had a rough life, but she had a nice shape.

"Why don't you give my girl a lap dance?"

"Lap dances are twenty-five dollars, and a private room is one hundred."

"Alright, let's see what you got out here first and then maybe we'll take it further," Rashod chuckled. The stripper danced all over Diamond, grabbing her breasts and rubbing up against her. Diamond was loving every bit of it and never imagined that another female could have her all hot and bothered, and the stripper knew that she was into it, too.

"So, how about that private room?," the stripper asked.

"I have another proposition for you," Rashod said. "How much do you charge for house calls?"

"What are you talking about?"

"I like what you do and so does my girl, so why don't we take this show to another level?"

"I'm still confused," the stripper said. Rashod pulled out a big wad of money and started counting it.

"Oh, you want a private show at your house with you and your girl?" Rashod nodded his head. "How much are you paying?"

"Give my girl your number and she'll call you with the details." The stripper handed Diamond a business card and gave her a wink of the eye as she walked away. Diamond looked at the card and it read: "Sexxy T, looking for a good time call me" and her number was underneath that with a naked lady with her legs open in the upper left corner.

"Man, that was easy," Diamond said.

"Yeah, sometimes you can get a lot by flashing a little bit of green."

"So, when are you trying to do this because I'm ready now?," Diamond asked.

"Hold your horses you little freak. Call ole' girl up and maybe we can get it set up for next weekend. Now, come on. Let's go home and relax for the rest of the evening."

The next morning, Rashod went to pick up the boys from Latifah's and Diamond wasted no time calling Sexxy T.
"Yeah?," Sexxy T answered in a sleepy voice.
"I'm sorry, did I wake you?," Diamond asked.
"Who is this?"
"This is Diamond, the girl from the club last night."
"Oh, hi you doing? No, I wasn't sleep. What's up?"
"Oh, nothing much, just checking out your business card. So, what do you consider a good time, I mean what do you do?"
"You saw me at work. I do whatever I have to do to feed my kids."
"Oh, really?"
"So, what's on your mind? Your man said he had some outside work he wanted to take care of so, what's up? I mean stop with the small talk and get to your reason for calling."
"I'm trying to get to know you and see where your head is at."
"You don't need to know me, this is all about business, if we're not talking about money then we don't need to talk at all."
"*This girl is a bitch.*" Diamond thought.
"Fine, my dude is looking for a chick to join us in the bedroom. Are you down or not?" Diamond couldn't believe how easily that had rolled off her tongue. Sexxy T smacked her lips. "Is that it? I charge one hundred and fifty dollars an hour and if I like what I'm getting, then I might give you some extra time for free."
"Cool, so when is a good time for you?"
"Well, I'm off on Tuesdays and Sundays but I go to church on Sundays and Tuesdays I take my kids out so whatever's good for you. I usually get off around two thirty. We can do it one night when I get off."

"That'll work, that way my kids will be sleep and I will have time to get myself right."

"So, what about next Friday night? That way, I can sleep in on Saturday because I'm also trying to do this school thing. That's why I'm working at the strip club. It's easy money and it pays the bills."

"So, do you do threesomes all the time or is this your first time?," Diamond asked.

"No, I don't do this all the time. Your dude is kind of cute and so are you. That outfit you had on was banging girl so keep in touch and if not, I'll see you next Friday around three A.M. Like I told you before, I work every day except for Tuesday and Sunday so come and see me sometime." They ended their call and Diamond felt like a new woman. She knew that her man would be proud.

CHAPTER - 21

Friday morning, Diamond got up and she, Rashod and the boys went to Country Skillet for breakfast because she had been craving some eggnog pancakes and she wanted the entire day to be perfect for her and her man. While they were eating, Diamond brought up the subject about Sexxy T.

"So, Rashod, I talked to ole' girl the other day."

"Who?," Rashod asked with a mouth full of pancakes.

"Miss T, you know."

"Oh," Rashod said with a smile. "What is she talking 'bout?"

"Tonight."

"For real?" Rashod was extra excited, and she could tell.

"So, I told her to come by when she gets off of work tonight, as a matter of fact, let me call her right now and give her the address." Diamond pulled out her cell phone and called Sexxy T.

"Hey, Diamond." She was surprised that Sexxy T knew who she was before she even said anything.

"Hey, Sexxy T. Is it still on for tonight?"

"I wouldn't miss the opportunity. I need some extra excitement in my life. Shit, I've been stressed to hell."

"I feel you, so let me give you my address." Sexxy T got a piece of paper.

"Okay, what's the address?" Diamond gave it to her. "So did you tell your man about my prices?"

"No, but he's willing to pay whatever to make our relationship better." Sexxy T laughed because she knew that this was not going to make things better; it would more than likely make things worse.

"Do you mind if I speak with him."

"No, hold on." She handed Rashod her cell phone.

"What's up, Sexxy?"

"First, turn down the phone. I know how loud cell phones can be." He turned down the phone. "So, are you ready for this?"
"You know it."
"I'm not trying to break up your happy home but I'm not an ordinary chick. I saw you checking me out when you first walked in the club. I make brothers want to leave their wives. I will charge you one hundred dollars an hour because I like you and Diamond's fat ass. I'm going to schedule you for three hours and the first hour is on me. I hope y'all can last the whole three hours and I hope you lay like you pay. That fifty-dollar tip you gave me at the club, let me know that you're about your business."
"You talk a good game. I hope you can back it up because Diamond is no amateur either and I've been around the block a few times myself, so you know." He was cheesing from ear to ear.
"Alright, I'll see y'all tonight and tell Diamond I'll call her when I'm on my way."
"I will and we'll see you soon." Rashod handed Diamond back her cell phone.
"What was that all about? I mean, what did she say?," Diamond asked.
"She said she'll call you when she's on her way."
"And what else?"
"She was just telling me how much she charged and stuff like that. Dang! Why are you so uptight?"
"Because first of all, you turned down the phone and y'all were on the phone for a minute." Rashod didn't think that Diamond had noticed him turning down the phone.
"I don't need everybody in this place in our business. Stop trippin' babe, she was just letting me know how she was going to rock your world." Diamond smiled visualizing what Sexxy T might do to her.
"So, what do you want me to wear?," Diamond asked.

"Do you still have that one little gown thing that shows that fat ass?"
"Rashod, the boys." Diamond said as she covered Brandon's ears.
"Oh, my fault." He lowered his tone to a whisper, "it shows those nice nipples."
"You're such a freak. Yes, I still have it and I got the thongs to match. And what are you going to wear?"
"Just some silk boxers and the matching robe."
"Do you think that your mom will watch the boys tonight?"
"I don't know, I told you she's been trippin' lately."
"Well, call her and ask please, because I don't want any interruptions or have to try to be quiet." Rashod called Latifah and she agreed to keep the boys as long as they picked them up first thing the next morning, and they agreed. Diamond went home and straightened up a little and got her outfit together, just in case, she needed to buy something to make everything right. She went through her closet and pulled out a pair of glass heels that Rashod hadn't torn up, laid everything on her dresser and she and the boys took a nap while Rashod ran some errands. He took Diamond's food stamp card, went to the grocery store and purchased some strawberries, cool whip, and popsicles. He used his money to buy some KY jelly, a six pack of beer and a bottle of that stuff that gets hot when you blow on it because he planned on having a good night. He went to spend some time with Sonya so she wouldn't bother him later and was home to Diamond by eight that evening, so they could drop the boys off at Latifah's and have time to get himself ready. When Rashod walked in the door, Diamond already had the boy's bags packed and ready to go. They dropped them off, went and got some King's Fried Chicken, came back home, got high and had a few drinks as they discussed the details for later that evening. Diamond told Rashod that everything goes, but he had to wear a condom and he wasn't allowed to perform oral sex on Sexxy T. He agreed,

as long as, Diamond promised to do what she had to do to make sure they were both satisfied, and she promised. At 2:45 A.M., Diamond's cell phone rang, and she knew it had to be Sexxy T, so she answered the phone in a sexy tone.

"Hello?"

"Hey Diamond, I'll be there in about ten minutes. I have to take a shower first." Diamond felt butterflies in her stomach, but it was too late to back out now, so she got up and put on her Victoria's Secret white negligee with matching thong and returned with her Baby Phat lotion as she sprayed a little Baby Phat perfume. Rashod was already, he had put on his clothes after they had finished their talk. They smoked another primo to get their heads clear of any doubts and they waited for Sexxy T.

CHAPTER - 22

Sexxy T arrived at 3:07 A.M. and Diamond was about to experience something she'd never thought that she would. Rashod answered the door with his maroon silk boxers and matching robe on, left open so that Sexxy T could see his well-kept physique. He had rubbed baby oil on his chest to make it look even more sexy.

"What's up baby? You are right on time. Come on in," Rashod said with a blunt hanging out of his mouth. She walked in with a long black jacket on that she had tied closed.

"Boy, do you look good. I can't wait to get this party started. Do y'all have anything to drink?," Sexxy T asked as she walked in.

"That's right, make yourself right at home. I have a bottle of Patron and a couple of Corona's. Do you want that on ice, with some juice or straight?"

"I don't like any dilution in my stuff, straight please." Sexxy T went into the kitchen to watch him make her drink.

"Where's your girl, Diamond?"

"Oh, she'll be down in a few minutes. She's freshening up or whatever y'all do." Sexxy T took her shot of Patron with one swallow.

"Can I have another shot, please? Give me one of those Corona's, too."

"Dang, you're a lush. You better slow down, this ain't no cheap liquor."

"You see where I work, I'm sure I can handle it. So, what do you have planned for me tonight?" Rashod rubbed his six pack and opened his robe.

"Baby, I'm going to give you something that you never had in your life, I'm sure by the end of the night you're going to want me to be your man." Sexxy T laughed and rolled her eyes. "I bought you some strawberries and wine so that I can feed you

and show you how a woman is supposed to be treated. I got some cherries so that I can..." and Rashod started moving his tongue in and out of his mouth like he was licking an ice cream cone. "Yeah, I know you're up on the popsicle game."
"Oh, so you're a super freak. I see why ole' girl is willing to do whatever it takes to make you happy." Diamond walked downstairs with her two-inch heel sandals on and her short negligee with the matching thong on. She had on make-up, was smelling and looking good, so good that Rashod had to take a second look.
"Oh, when did you get her?," Diamond asked.
"Not too long ago, just had enough time to have a quick shot or two. Wow! You look real nice," Sexxy T said.
"Yes, you do baby. Damn! I got two sexy ladies in one room and tonight y'all both belong to me. Y'all ready to get this party started?," Rashod asked as he gathered the strawberries, cherries and popsicles.
"As ready as ever," Sexxy T said as she got up out of the chair.
"Well, follow me," Diamond said as she headed upstairs.
"Hold up baby. Diamond, let's do it how we did when we first met."
"Rashod, what are you talking about?"
"T, why don't you put on a little show for us to get us in the mood?"
"That sounds good so everybody can be relaxed, and we won't be rushing into anything." Diamond put on some slow, but freaky music and Sexxy T started grinding the air and shaking her butt. She took her jacket off and was wearing a Victoria's Secret black negligee, almost like Diamond's and the matching thong. Sexxy T's, looked better on her because she had a bigger butt and a smaller waist. She went over to where Rashod was sitting on the couch, put her leg up on his shoulder and started popping her vagina in his face. He laid back with a big smile on his face. She bent over and shook her

butt in his face, and he smacked her on it. She finished her Corona and set the bottle on the floor, turned her back to Diamond and Rashod and slowly bounced her butt up and down as she lowered her body to the floor. She hurdled over the Corona bottle and let it go inside of her vagina as she did a split, she went so low that the label on the bottle disappeared. Sexxy T looked to see if she was turning him on and the front of his boxer shorts were wet so she knew she was doing her thing. Rashod had never seen any girl put on a performance like that, not even in a strip club, and he couldn't wait to get Sexxy T to his bedroom. Diamond was amazed at her, also but she was angry that her man couldn't take his eyes off Sexxy T. Diamond went over, sat on Rashod's lap and began to kiss him in the mouth.

"Hey, remember me?," she asked in a low but sarcastic tone.

"Baby don't start trippin' I'm really enjoying myself. Why don't you go over there and dance with her? That will really make it right." Diamond got up and started dancing like a stripper, she had watched plenty of movies and had watched Sexxy T and her friends the night they had met.

"Aww shit, go Diamond," Sexxy T said as she watched Diamond shake her butt. "You need to come down to the club and work with me. We can make some real money as a team." Diamond smiled as she continued to dance, she had planned on going to the club and putting in an application. She bent over to give Rashod something to look at and Sexxy T got behind her and started grinding on her. She was cool with that and was even grinding back so Sexxy T grabbed her vagina, kissed her on the back of her neck and Diamond froze. She tried to walk away but Sexxy T walked in front of her and started kissing her lips. Diamond was kissing her back but when Sexxy T stuck her tongue in her mouth, Diamond turned her head. She wasn't feeling this, anymore.

"I can't do this." Diamond walked away from her.

"What's wrong, Boo?," Sexxy T asked.

“I’m just a little nervous, that’s all. I’ve never done this before.”
“Lay down on the couch, I got something that will grab your attention.” Sexxy T went into the kitchen and motioned for Rashod to follow her.
“Where are the popsicles that you said you bought? We got to get this girl to relax or she’s going to cop out. I’ve seen this happen one time too many.” Rashod opened the freezer, grabbed the banana popsicles and handed one to Sexxy T. She opened it as she headed back to the living room where Diamond was lying on the couch with her arm over her forehead, one leg bent and the other one over the side of the couch. Sexxy T grabbed the bent leg, opened it up and Diamond let her leg fall. Sexxy T kissed her between her legs as Rashod kissed her in the mouth. Diamond relaxed because she was face to face with her man. Sexxy T inserted the popsicle inside of Diamond and licked away the melting banana juices. Diamond just laid there for a few seconds, moaning softly because it felt really good. It was weird, though, nothing like she had ever felt before. It froze her but the softness of Sexxy T’s lips warmed her back up. Diamond was enjoying it until she remembered it was another woman that was making her feel so good and she jumped up.
“Hold up! This just ain’t right.”
“What’s wrong? That don’t feel good to you?”
“It does but another woman should not be making me feel like this.”
“Relax, baby and visualize me between those legs and enjoy what this young lady is doing to you. I saw how you were all into it for a minute, so I know she was making you feel good.”
“Yeah, it did feel good, but this is just not me. I’m sorry I wasted your time, but I can’t go through with this.” Sexxy T looked at Rashod, who was shaking his head in disgust. Sexxy T sat there and thought for a moment, she went and got her jacket and pulled a pill bottle out of her pocket. She opened

the bottle and took out two ecstasy pills, put one in her mouth and handed the other one to Rashod while nodding her head toward Diamond, signaling for him to give her the pill. He already knew what it was, he put the pill in his mouth, kissed Diamond in hers and then pushed the pill in her mouth.

"Swallow it, baby."

"What is this?," Diamond asked.

"Something to make you relax. You had me all pumped and now you're letting me down." Diamond swallowed the pill because she wanted to make her man happy. This was hard for her because she had never been with another girl, and it felt weird. She laid there while Rashod and Sexxy T laid on the couch freaking each other. They knew that she would come around in a little while. Sexxy T was lying on top of Rashod kissing him in the mouth and massaging his chest while she was grinding on his erection. Diamond jumped up off the couch.

"What the fuck are you doing? I told you not to kiss her in the mouth! I don't want to do this shit, anymore. Bitch, get the fuck out of my house!" She started throwing pillows from the couch at them.

"Go over there and get her in the mood," Sexxy T said to Rashod. "Sometimes people wild out, then they get in the mood." He got up, grabbed Diamond and kissed her on the lips as he gripped her butt, he backed her up to the wall and put her arms up over her head while kissing her passionately. He picked her up and she wrapped her legs around his waist, feeling his erect penis touching her butt, then she began to kiss him back while rubbing the back of his head. Rashod carried Diamond upstairs and signaled for Sexxy T to follow. He laid Diamond on the bed and performed oral sex on her until she was almost there while Sexxy T massaged his manhood.

"Come on, baby. Go finish getting Diamond right." Sexxy T did just that and then she started to work on Rashod and pleased him while Diamond pleased her. Sexxy T was a pro at what she was doing, she was sucking him like she was sucking a golf ball through a water hose. Rashod felt the tears fill up in his eyes as he came multiple times and although he agreed not to, he had to return the favor. Rashod pleased Sexxy T and she pleased Diamond until she tapped out and fell asleep. Rashod and Sexxy T finished the last half an hour with each other. He paid her two hundred dollars, and they exchanged numbers so that they could hook up again, without Diamond.

Later that afternoon, Diamond called Sexxy T to make sure that Rashod had paid her, that she had enjoyed her evening and told her that she would love to see her again without Rashod and she agreed.

Diamond and Sexxy T began to see each other on a regular basis as a couple, Sexxy T agreed to let Diamond continue seeing Rashod because she had him first, unknown to Diamond that she was seeing him, also so they both were living the life they wanted. Sexxy T would pick up Diamond and she would tell Rashod they were going shopping. Sexxy T bought Diamond all kinds of lingerie and would give her ideas on what to buy for Rashod so she could see him in it, too. They would leave the mall and go back to Sexxy T's house in Clarksdale, Arizona. She had inherited the house from her late parents who were killed in a car accident by a drunk driver. It was just about paid for because she used some of the money they left her to make sure she would never lose the home they had worked so hard to get. It has three bedrooms, a bathroom with a jacuzzi connected to her room, all of the appliances in the kitchen is GE stainless steel and art is Vincent Van Gough. She had taken dance lessons and gymnastics since she was four years old so doing splits and back bends was nothing to her.

When Diamond saw Sexxy T's house, she thought: "*stripping must be paying some good money for her to be able to afford a crib like this. Wow, everything's spotless for her to have a child,"* but she didn't ask. Sexxy T would put Diamond in so many different sexual positions that Diamond never wanted to leave her. She turned Diamond out and Diamond was in love with another woman, something she'd never imagined would happen to her, but she still loved Rashod because he did things to her that another woman just couldn't do, not even with a strap on, it just wasn't the same.

One afternoon, Diamond and Rashod were supposed to meet at 12:30 P.M. at Goodale Park for a romantic picnic but he hadn't shown up. It was one and she had to pick up her boys from daycare before five and she wanted to have plenty of time for their love making. She called Rashod's cell phone several times and continued to get his voicemail so by two o'clock, she was pissed because he hadn't returned any of her calls. "*Forget him! I'm tired of always waiting around for this clown! I'm so glad that I met Sexxy T. I'm going to spend some time with my new Boo. She knows how to satisfy me real quick and I'll still have time to go pick up my boys."* Diamond changed her clothes from her Old Navy sundress to a pair of Ecko Red booty blue jean shorts, a green tank top and some green flip flops, went to the store to purchase some banana popsicles and cherries because those were games she really enjoyed playing with Sexxy T. It felt weird but it made her cum multiple times and that's what she needed right now, to release some of her stress. Diamond got into her freshly waxed Sebring, rims glowing and looked for a "fuck'em" CD and came across Trina, just what she needed. She put it in the player and turned her 15-inch woofers up to number twelve which is just loud enough to rattle people's windows when she rode by. She called Sexxy T to let her know that she was on her way, but she got her voicemail. She figured she must still be asleep, considering she had worked the night before and had to go to school that morning, so she was probably tired, and she was going to surprise her. She took the thirty-minute drive to her house and lifted the flowerpot for the key, but it wasn't there, so she knocked on the front door, but no one answered. She looked in the side door of Sexxy T's garage and her 2007 silver Cadillac Escalade was there, so she knew she had to be home. She tried knocking again and even rang the doorbell but still there was no answer, so she called her phone again and again and continued to get her voicemail. She walked around to the side of the house to knock on Sexxy T's bedroom window and saw Rashod's Cadillac parked on the street. She looked in the window and saw him holding her up against the wall, her legs were wrapped around his waist and her arms around his neck while stroking the back of his head. The window was ajar, and she heard 'Sex Me' by R. Kelly playing so Diamond could barely hear them but from the look on Sexxy T's face and the sweat on Rashod's back, they both were enjoying each other. She bammed on the window but they didn't stop. She wanted to throw a brick or something through the window, but her yard was so well kept that she couldn't find anything. Diamond looked around and found a flowerpot sitting on the patio, picked it up and threw it through the window and they slowed down but didn't stop. She was about to slash Rashod's tires, but she didn't have anything to do it with. Diamond was tired of all this drama, maybe her mother was right; she needed a change in her life and a trip to Ohio might do her some good. She slowly walked to her car, dropping the cherries and popsicles in the grass. When she got in her car she sat there, rolled herself a blunt and thought: "*I can't be mad at anyone but myself.*" *All I was trying to do was keep my man happy and now, not only am I hurt by one person, but two. I no longer want to go on with my life.*" When Diamond got home, she went to Rashod's stash, smoked what she could smoke and popped a couple of pills. She was so high that all she could see was little black spots, but she was so numb that she couldn't even cry about Rashod and Sexxy T, so she laid down on the couch and fell asleep.

When she woke up, Rosetta was holding Deontae' and Rashod was standing over her.
"Diamond, are you alright? Baby, I've been calling you for a couple of hours. I was so worried about you. The boys and I were sitting in the driveway when Rashod pulled up," Rosetta said. Diamond opened her eyes, trying to remember if she was dreaming about Sexxy T and Rashod or if it was real. She looked at Rashod and then reality hit her.
"You dirty bastard! How are you going to fuck with my girl? Yeah, I came to her house and saw y'all all up on the wall. Y'all can have each other because I've made up my mind, I'm leaving!" She tried to get up from the couch, but she had a splitting headache. "Oh my gosh!," Diamond screamed as she grabbed her forehead, covering the light from her eyes.
"Rashod, thanks for letting me in but it's time for you to go. Every time I come around here, you got Diamond all distraught and frustrated. You got her on these damn drugs! Look at her!"
"Ma'am, I didn't do anything to Diamond. I don't even know what she's talking about."
"I'm sure you don't. Go ahead and see yourself out before I call the police." Rashod was cool with that because he didn't really want to stay with Diamond that night anyway. He had made love to Sexxy T for most of the afternoon and although they had taken a short nap, he was still totally exhausted. She was no joke. The girl had mad skills and he couldn't be falling for this fine girl with a banging body, a nice crib, a job, only one kid, some change in her pocket and someone who was trying to better themselves by going to college. Diamond and Sexxy T were like night and day, but they were freaky.

Diamond was there for him mentally, she made him feel the way that Sonya had for years but Sexxy T fulfilled all of his physical needs; he didn't have to say anything to her, she could ride him for a good hour, giving it to him without drying out or even getting tired, he could put her in any position and she wouldn't complain, she even put him in a few. No female had ever satisfied him like this, and he never thought that he would find a girl freakier than Diamond. He didn't want to lose either one but if he had to choose, he was going to choose Sexxy T, no doubt.

That evening, Diamond called her father Brian in Columbus, Ohio and made arrangements to stay with him the following week. Rosetta got on the internet, found a rehab in Columbus and signed Diamond up. She agreed to go as soon as she got off the train. She agreed to leave her food stamp card with her mom since she was keeping her kids. She also agreed to give her father one hundred dollars a month for food because she needed some junk food. Brian was joyful to have Diamond stay with him, he hadn't seen her in over ten years. He sent her a one-way train ticket and she packed all of her clothes, personal items and put the rest of her things in storage, which Rosetta agreed to pay for until she returned. She spent the next couple of days with her kids by taking them everywhere she could afford and buying them anything they wanted because she knew the first was coming soon and she would be getting another check. All she wanted was for her kids to remember a good time with her. Rashod hadn't come around to see Diamond or her kids, but she didn't care, she had packed all his things and took them to Latifah's. She gave her a hug and just walked away without saying a word. Rashod didn't think Diamond was really leaving but this time, he was in for a big surprise.

CHAPTER - 23

When Diamond arrived in Ohio, she was surprised as to how cold it was. She wasn't dressed for this; she had on a pair of black capris and a white tank top, and it had to be at least forty degrees outside. Her father told her that it was chilly, but she thought that he meant Arizona chilly, like seventy degrees. Diamond went into her Coach bag and grabbed another shirt that would at least cover her shoulders and waited for her father to pick her up. Diamond and Brian quickly bonded, they went to a steak house downtown to eat as soon as she got off the train, they talked and laughed. She told him all about her kids, how bad her boys were and how controlling her mother is.

"Yeah baby, I know just how your mother is. She's crazy and I hope you have my genes because if not, we're not going to be able to live together." Brian started to laugh. "Boy, some of the memories I have about your mother, baby, I could tell you some stories."

"I could only imagine, and I could tell you some, too. Brian I have lived a crazy life and the past two years have been totally crazy. I need to talk to somebody that's not going to judge me. That's been my problem and why I finally left. My mother has changed a lot, but she always judged me and that's why I moved out of her house. I don't feel like I have anyone to talk to. My sister, Regina and I have never been close and ever since she moved to Colorado with her man, Joe, she doesn't really communicate with the family. She comes home maybe once every five years, but she acts so uppity that I don't really fool with her. She always has something to say about my kids, the places that I stay and the company that I keep. I know I'm not perfect and I'm not going to try to be, and Timothy, well, that's a whole 'nother story."

"Baby girl, all you can do is be yourself. Don't let anyone try to make you who you're not. If you respect yourself then the people around you will have no choice but to respect you too, and if they don't, then you don't need to be around them."

"OK, you say that, but I am supposed to respect my mother and she never showed me any respect." Brian laughed because he knows exactly how Rosetta is.

"You're supposed to respect your mother, but you have your own house, so you only have to deal with her for so long. But you're here with me, right now so maybe your life will be a little different, at least, for a little while." They finished their steak dinners and went back to his one-bedroom apartment. Diamond was amazed as to how small the apartments were compared to hers in Cottonwood, Arizona. They didn't even have a pool, but it was quiet and, so far, she hadn't seen any gecko's running around, because she hated those things.

Diamond and Brian got along great; she went to rehab but only stayed for a few days. It just wasn't for her, and she thought that she was cured that fast. She and the girl next door, Chrissy, became close friends and she told her where the weed was and from there, Diamond was able to get all the drugs that she needed but all she did was pop a few pills here and there. Brian was nothing like Rosetta, he knew what was going on and made sure that Diamond stayed busy.

"So, Diamond, what do you want to do with your life? I go to work driving a truck every day and you need to find something to occupy your time."

"Well, I want to go to school but I don't know what I want to do."

"Well, nursing is a good field and in eighteen months, you can be certified and maybe find a job. I mean, I don't know how long you plan on staying here, but at least you can get something started." They went to Nurse Institute and got her registered. She was able to get financial aid so that gave her a free ride and money in her pocket after she bought her books.

Brian didn't make Diamond pay any bills or do anything else as long as she cleaned up after herself and kept her grades up which was cool with her. She had written Vonte' and apologized for not being there for him as she promised and told him about some of the things that she and Rashod had been through. She gave him her new address if he wanted to keep in touch. Brian agreed to let Vonte' call twice a month, as long as Diamond was doing something with her life, and she had to pay the phone bill. James' lady friend named Pam, gave her a job as an intern at the Medical Hospital until she finished school so she would have experience. This kept Diamond busy and not a lot of time to think about getting high, she still did, but not as much and popped a few pills but she could still function. She wasn't sexing every guy like she had in Arizona. Her male friend, Todd kept her company when she was lonely. She was just enjoying her freedom and life, in general.

Diamond decided that she would finish school in Ohio, so once a month she would fly home to see her kids and spend a few days with them, even if she missed school. Eighteen months went by extremely fast, and Rosetta and her grandkids packed up in Diamond's Sebring and drove to Ohio for Diamond's graduation. Rosetta was proud Diamond was staying in Ohio, she had accomplished more in eighteen months then she had in the past six years and Rosetta was very proud of her daughter. Mario was glad that his little cousin had finally gotten her life together, he couldn't make it to the graduation because he was giving free haircuts to some of the kids that he worked with, but he did send a five hundred dollar check inside of a card. Diamond was so shocked that she almost cried when she saw Regina and her husband, Joe walks through the door. She didn't think she cared about her.

She was so glad to have her family together, she had really missed her mother and her kids, although she was stress free, she wanted her kids back. She was a little disappointed that Timothy couldn't make it because he was given a job as Mario's assistant, and they were together. She had spoken to Rashod on a couple of occasions, but she realized that he was no good for her and was glad that he couldn't contact her nor come and see her to manipulate her and make her feel as if she needed him. Diamond walked across the stage and cried when they handed her, her Nursing Certification. She never really thought she would finish but Brian showed interest and would help her study in the evenings by quizzing her on what she learned in school and with his lady friend, Pam being a nurse, she helped her, also. She graduated in the top ten of her class. She and her family went to dinner at The Steak House downtown to celebrate.

The next week, Diamond was hired into the hospital as an LPN. Rosetta had been staying in a hotel enjoying the city while Diamond spent time with her kids, and she decided to leave her grandkids and Diamond's Sebring in Ohio and catch a plane back home to Cottonwood by herself. Diamond was cool with that because she had her life together, even though she didn't have a place to stay, but had a good job and in time, she'd have a nice place for her family. Brian didn't mind his grandchildren staying with him, it was summertime, and they could do a lot. Nikki was thirteen and able to babysit her brothers, so Brian and Diamond were able to go to work and not worry about having to pay for daycare or finding someone to watch the kids.

Diamond worked for two and a half months without missing a day and in two weeks, she would pass her probationary period and be hired with benefits and get a raise.

One afternoon, Diamond had taken blood from Ms. Janet Smith, one of her patients, and was putting the needle into the full hazardous box when she tried to push it in, she pricked her finger.
"Oh shit!," Diamond yelled while pulling off her glove and looking at her finger, just as nosey nurse, Mirna was walking into the room.
"What happened Diamond?," Mirna asked.
"Oh nothing," Diamond said as she pulled her hand behind her back.
"Did you poke your finger with one of those needles?"
"No, I'm alright."
"You better go and get that checked out."
"It's nothing, I said I am alright."
"I'm going to go ahead and write up an accident report because you can be infected with something. These people are in here for a reason and if you got something, it would be best to take care of it now before it gets worse."
"I just got hired. I don't want to lose my job."
"Would you rather be sick and die? Then you still won't have a job. All they're going to do is give you a blood test to make sure everything is alright, I had one before and it's nothing."
"Whatever." Diamond was upset and was wishing Mirna hadn't walked into the room because her life was going so well. Five minutes later, Diamond was called to the office by her supervisor, Roxanne. Diamond took her time trying to think of a way to get out of this. She walked into her office.
"Hello Roxanne." Diamond said with a smile.
"What happened? Mirna told me that you poked your finger with a needle in the hazardous box. Are you alright?"
"I'm fine, Roxanne. I had on gloves, and I didn't get hurt."
"Alright, you were doing like you were supposed to."
"Yeah, someone didn't empty the box last night and I didn't realize it was full."
"Did you bleed?"

"Just a little, like I said it was nothing serious. I put a little pressure on it, and it stopped in like two seconds."
"Well, let me see your finger." Roxanne looked at her finger and didn't see anything. "You appear to be fine, but I would feel more comfortable if you got the blood work done because if you don't and something goes wrong in the future, I don't want to be responsible."
"Roxanne, I don't want to lose my job. I'm not even hired in yet."
"You are so cute. Don't worry about that, you haven't done anything wrong but the person that worked last night will get wrote up for not emptying that box." Roxanne scribbled something on a piece of paper. "Here, take this to the lab and get your lab work done, I'll allow you to stay on the clock, just hurry up. I need it before you leave today." Diamond was done. She went back into Ms. Smith's room hoping to use some of her blood.
"Hey, are you sleeping?," Diamond asked with a smile.
"No, I'm just lying here. Is everything alright?," Ms. Smith asked.
"No, I have to go get a blood test. I hate needles." She really didn't mind them, she had several tattoos, she just didn't want to do it. "You don't do drugs, or anything do you?," Diamond asked.
"Why are you asking me that?"
"I don't know, I'm trippin'."
"You want to use my blood, don't you? Well, I'm going to be honest with you, I have dibbed and dabbed a little bit and if you put that in my charts, I'll tell that you asked to use my blood."
"I wouldn't play you like that." Diamond thought: *"forget it."* She went and got her blood work done.

Two weeks had passed, and Diamond figured she was in the clear. Roxanne called her into her office and when she walked in, Roxanne's boss, Mrs. Laura Brown was sitting at the table, too. Diamond smiled as she sat down because she was positive that they were calling her into the office to hire her in and give her a raise. She sat down at the table with her notepad.

"Alright Diamond, I'm not going to keep you too long. You would've been here ninety days today, but ..." Roxanne glanced at Mrs. Brown who nodded her head for her to continue. Diamond started to fidget in her seat.

"Well Diamond, we got your blood work back last week and marijuana and some prescription drugs were detected in your system. They were not prescribed to you by a doctor, so unfortunately, we're going to have to let you go. Al, the security guard is outside the door and will accompany you while you clean out your locker to leave the premises."

"You're firing me? I've worked so hard for the past year and a half to get certified, and this is what I get?" Diamond began to cry. "My life is never going to change! Can't you send me to rehab or something to get some help?"

"If you were a full-time employee when all of this happened, that would've been an option, but unfortunately, it's not at this time." Diamond got up from the table devastated. She didn't know what she was going to do. Brian was so proud of her because she'd been doing so well, he was not going to be happy now. She had been able to buy her kids everything that they needed and more and she enjoyed getting up going to work every morning. She gathered her things, irritated while Al stood over her.

Diamond went to Goodale Park and smoked a blunt while she fed the ducks to try to clear her mind and think of what she was going to do to take care of her kids. She was back to square one. She still received twenty percent of her social security so that's considered income. She wasn't trying to get back into the system because she finally saw what it was like to have real money and be able to do whatever she wanted, whenever she wanted and not just at the beginning of the month. She knew Brian would help her, but she was almost thirty years old, it was time for her to be an adult, take care of herself and her own kids. Vonte' only had a year and a half left and she wanted things altogether when he came home so that they could be a family, again. Vonte' was so proud of Diamond that he even made her a nice graduation gift in one of his craft classes in prison. It was a plaque that read: "Congratulations, you did it. I will always love you for the person you are. Love, Vonte'." Diamond hung it over her bed to see it every morning when she got up and every night before she went to bed and that's one thing that kept her motivated. Vonte' had promised her that he would get a job, no matter what it paid as soon as he was released and as a team they would do well. Diamond had to figure out what her next step would be now.

CHAPTER - 24

Diamond decided that she was not going to tell Brian right away that she had lost her job. She still had one more paycheck coming, and she was hoping by then she would have a new job. Every morning, she would go to a pancake place, because almost all restaurant has Wi-Fi, free internet, and sit at a booth with her laptop and look through the classified ads and apply for jobs. She would leave her cell phone close by so employers could contact her wherever she was, and Brian wouldn't know.

Three days had passed, Diamond hadn't heard from anyone, and everyday Brian wanted to know how her day at work went, like he had from day one, and she had to make up some stories. She hated to lie to her father, but she didn't know what else to do. Finally, she decided to go to Temp to Hire, a temporary agency and she had no problem getting hired on the spot since she had a degree. The only problem was, she had to pass the drug test. The job paid two dollars an hour less from what she was making at the Medical Hospital, but she didn't care, it was still decent money. Diamond went home, earlier than usual because she had to take the drug test before she could start, and the place closed at five that evening. When she walked in the house, she was amazed as to how well-behaved her kids were. Nikki was fixing the boys chicken nuggets and French fries for lunch, Deontae' was asleep while Brandon and Lil' Vonte' were sitting down watching cartoons. Diamond walked into the living room, kissed her boys, she went into the dining room and sat down at the table so that she could talk to Nikki.
"Nikki, I need you to do me a favor."
"What's up, Mom?" Diamond sighed heavily while Nikki came and sat at the table with her. "Mom, what's wrong?"

Diamond hated to ask her daughter to do this but she felt as if she had no other choice.
"Nikki, I need some of your pee."
"What?" The look on her face made Diamond laugh.
"I need you to pee in a cup for me."
"What do you need that for? You trying to find out who my dad is or something? I'm almost grown now, and I really don't care who he is."
"Girl, it's nothing like that. Your crazy butt." Diamond laughed again. She really had missed her kids, they always cheered her up when she was down.
"Well, what do you need it for?"
"Alright, I lost my job the other day because I got hurt on the job and wasn't able to pass the drug test." Nikki rolled her eyes at her mother.
"You get us all the way out here and then you start messing up, again?"
"Baby, it's not like that. Somebody forgot to empty the hazardous box and I was poked by a dirty needle. They had to make sure that I didn't get some kind of disease or something."
"Wow! Are you alright?"
"I'm fine but I got a new job today and I have to pass this drug test."
"What have you been doing that you can't use your own?"
"Well, I'll be honest with you, I've been a little down and I'm not using this as an excuse, but I smoked a little weed and stuff to help clear my head."
"What kind of stuff? Isn't that why you had to go to rehab?" Nikki knew everything that had gone on in her mother's life because Rosetta always walked around the house talking to herself and complaining about Diamond when she was upset. Nikki would always end up sitting in the room and listening.
"Baby, I had some other issues that I resolved. I'm not a junkie, if that's what you're asking. I just need your help right

now so that we can move out of this one-bedroom apartment and get our own place."

"Um..." Nikki turned in her chair and was no longer facing her mother.

"Are you going to do it or not?"

"I guess I have no choice." Diamond went in their room, got a sterilized bottle that she had taken from the Medical Hospital and gave it to Nikki. "I don't have to pee right now."

"Come on Nikki. I need this before five o'clock." She took the container and went into the bathroom and tried. She was able to give her a little bit, enough to reach the number two on the bottle. Diamond kissed her daughter as she headed out the door.

"Thanks babe, I love you and this better come back negative." She put the container in her glove compartment so it could stay warm and headed to the drug testing building. She pulled into the parking lot, took the container out of her glove compartment, put it in her underwear and put on her smock so no one would notice the little bulge. There was only one person ahead of her, so she was in and out in less than twenty minutes. She went home, sent her kids to the park that's behind their apartment and laid down on the couch and began to cry. She felt like a failure. Brian walked into the house carrying some groceries and heard his daughter sobbing as he set the bags on the counter. He peeked into the living room, saw Diamond on the couch, put up the milk and the freezer food, leaving out chicken, broccoli and cheese, corn on the cob and biscuits that he was making for dinner and went into the living room and sat on the edge of the couch rubbing Diamond's back.

"What's the matter baby?" Diamond sat up and wiped the tears from her face.

"Dad, I feel like a loser." She hadn't called Brian Dad since she was a little girl.

"Why? What happened?"

"I lost my job the other day and I was too ashamed that I didn't tell you. I got all the way up here to get nowhere. I was doing so well, and somebody else's mistake caused me to lose my job."

"What do you mean? You didn't try to fight it?"

"Well, it was my fault, too, if I would've stopped getting high then I would have been alright."

"I don't understand, you always appeared to be in your right mind. I noticed you sleeping a lot, but I figured you were just tired from working. The rehab didn't work, and how did that make you lose your job?"

"The rehab did work a little bit. I mean, I'm not on any heavy drugs. I guess I just like the feeling of being high because it makes me relax and puts me to sleep. A little bit of weed never hurt anyone." Diamond smiled.

"How did they find out?"

"Someone at work didn't empty thc hazardous box. I was poked by a dirty needle, and I had to get tested."

"That's messed up. So, do you smoke because you're stressed out here? That sounds like a lot of excuses to me."

"No, to be honest, that's just what I like to do and now look at my life. Nikki thinks I'm a loser and so do you now." She began to cry, again. "Dad, I appreciate everything that you've done for my kids and me but it's a little tight in here with six of us in a one-bedroom apartment. I want my own place."

"I understand that. I mean, who's grown that don't want to be on their own? I'm going to tell you what, you need to take it to the rock, baby. The Lord is your foundation and if you go to Him for help, I'm quite sure He'll answer you. It may not be today or tomorrow, but He'll come on time. Maybe the job wasn't right for you because everything happens for a reason." Brian kissed Diamond on her forehead and went to start dinner. Diamond thought about what her father had said, got up from the couch and went to Goodale Park to relax in peace and have a long talk with God. She wanted to stop smoking

weed, get a good job and a place of her own to raise her kids. After about an hour of relaxing, she got into her Sebring and headed home. Just as she was leaving the parking lot, her cell phone rang, and an unknown number came across the screen.
"Hello?," Diamond answered.
"Hello, may I speak with Diamond?"
"Speaking."
"Hi Diamond. This is Tammy from Temp to Hire."
"Oh, hi Tammy."
"We just received everything you need to start your new job. Can you start Monday at eight A.M.?"
"I will be there at seven forty-five." She was so happy that she thanked God, went home and ate the dinner that Brian had made while she told them the good news. Diamond went next door to Chrissy's, smoked a blunt with her and then took her kids to the water park because she wanted to celebrate.

Diamond's job at State Hospital worked out perfect. She worked ninety days and was hired in. She found her and the kids a four-bedroom house not too far from her father.

Six months later, Vonte' was released from prison. Diamond couldn't get him because she hadn't accumulated that many vacation days, yet so she gave him a few days to spend with his mother, Vanessa and sister Valerie in Phoenix, Arizona and then she sent him a train ticket. Vonte' packed everything he could in his huge suitcase and headed to Ohio, he missed his woman and his boys. Diamond didn't take the kids with her to pick him up because she wanted all his attention. She was so happy to see her man that she cried when he stepped off the train. They embraced and kissed for at least three minutes without taking a breath. Vonte' had on a white tank top that showed off his big muscular arms and a pair of khaki shorts that showed all the muscles in his calves, prison had done him very well. She was so excited to take

Vonte' to their new home because she wanted to show him the progress that she had made since he had been on 'a state paid vacation' and he was impressed.
"Damn baby, this is a nice crib. How're you able to afford this by yourself?"
"Baby, I have a good job and nothing illegal."
"And look at my boys." Vonte's eyes filled with tears because this was the first time he had seen his son Deontae' and Vonte' Jr. was a splitting image of him. He was a little baby when he went to prison. They gave him a hug because Diamond had showed them pictures of him and told them that he was their father, but they didn't know him. Vonte' spent the whole evening with his boys, playing with them until they fell asleep and then he and Diamond made up for five years of lost time. She was hurt when Vonte' took off his shirt and saw that the tattoo of her name that was on his chest had been blacked out, but she understood, she had done him wrong.

Vonte' wasn't going to let his woman do everything by herself anymore, the first week he was home, he relaxed and then he went looking for a job. He wasn't having much luck, so Diamond called Tammy from Temp to Hire and told her that her man was new in town and really needed a job. He was willing to do anything.

The following morning, Vonte' went to see Tammy and she was impressed with all the skills that he had, she didn't know that he had obtained them in prison but what difference did it make? Tammy got Vonte' a job at Motor Company and he operated the machines to make parts for cars. After doing five years in prison, it felt good to be able to get up every morning, go to work doing something he enjoyed and getting paid for it. Vonte' agreed to pay the mortgage and all Diamond had to do was pay the utilities and buy the groceries. They went half, or took turns, buying the kids what they needed so no one was doing more than the other. They put Vonte Jr. and Deontae' in daycare, Nikki and Brandon were in private school and they split the cost of these expenses. Vonte' treated Nikki and Brandon as if they were his own children. Earl kept in contact with Nikki and sent her money once a month because to him, she was still his daughter. Stephon went to jail for domestic violence against his baby mama, the one who he was chillin' with when Diamond called to talk to him about Nikki when she was a baby. She found out that he was Nikki's father, but she didn't push the issue because she had Vonte' and they were happy. She wasn't going to force anyone to take care of their child. God had made her able to take care of her own and with her man's help, she was doing just fine.

CHAPTER - 25

Friday morning, Diamond got up humming and singing because it was her thirtieth birthday and she had been at the State Hospital for two years. She was due for her annual raise this week and since it was the last day of the week, it had to be today. Diamond and Vonte' had a nice savings account since they both were able to save two checks a month plus her social security check and they were scheduled to pick up his dark blue, 2006 Chevy Tahoe when she got from work. They decided to pay cash because both of their credit was shaky, and they didn't want a high car payment.

Diamond arrived at work fifteen minutes early like she did every day, sat at her desk and paid her bills and balanced her checkbook while checking her account online until it was time for her to clock in. She noticed that the account was one thousand dollars short, so she called State Bank and was told that Vonte' had withdrawn the money last week. She didn't want to call him right away because she didn't want her coworkers in her business so she figured she would talk to him when she got off.

Diamond only received a twenty cent raise but she was cool with that. One of her coworkers brought her a yellow cake decorated in pastel colors, it was delicious and when she returned from lunch, she had a beautiful vase with eleven roses on her desk and a stuffed monkey attached. She looked for the card to see who they were from, and it read: *There is only eleven roses because twelve is common and the last one is somewhere you'll never imagine. Happy Birthday. I love you baby. Your man Vonte'. Hurry home!*

Diamond had never received flowers at work before and her head was big for the rest of the afternoon. She couldn't wait until four thirty. She rushed to her car leaving her flowers on her desk so she could look at them on Monday morning and be reminded of how good her man is. As soon as Diamond got into her car, her cell phone rang.

"Hello."

"Hey love, you don't have to go and pick up the kids, I already got that handled for you to make your day easier," Vonte' said.

"Oh yeah?," she asked with a smile.

"I figured since I was off today than I could help you out a little bit."

"I appreciate that. Where are they?"

"Don't worry about that, just hurry home."

"I'll see you soon." She hung up the phone and was glad that she made amends with her man. "*What the hell was I thinking going to Rashod and leaving my man? I must've been out of my damn mind. Thank you, Jesus for letting me get my man back. He's the best thing that ever happened to me," Diamond* thought aloud. She pulled in the driveway and Vonte' was standing there. He ran in the house, locked the door and ran back to her Sebring.

"Move over."

"What are you doing?," Diamond asked.

"Let's go, I'm ready to pick up my truck and I figured we'd go and get something to eat."

"Can I at least freshen up a little?"

"Baby, you're fine." Diamond rolled her eyes as she put the car in park so Vonte could get in.

"Get out the way I'm driving," he said.

"Where are my kids?"

"They're with your father."

"Oh, really? Where are we going?"

"Just sit back and enjoy the ride." Diamond did just that. They went to the car lot, dropped six thousand dollars on

Vonte's truck, he followed her home to drop off her car and then she got into his truck. Vonte' pulled in the parking lot of Burger Place and Diamond just looked at him. He parked his truck and she just sat there.

"Are you getting out or what?"

"Man, you're tripping. I know you're not taking me here for my birthday." Vonte' continued to walk into the restaurant and Diamond followed.

"What do you want?"

"Nothing," she said with an attitude.

"Alright, let me get three cheeseburgers, a double cheeseburger, two small fries, two medium fries and um... you sure you don't want anything?" He started smiling because he knew that she was pissed. "Let me get three small orange pops and two medium cokes."

"Is that for here or to go?," the young lady asked. Vonte' looked at Diamond who turned her back to him.

"Make it to go. Man, she trippin'. "They got into the truck, Diamond had tears in her eyes because her day had been going so well and this was how he was going to do her.

"It's a thousand dollars missing out of our account, where is it?" Vonte' looked at her and started laughing.

"Are you bringing that up because you're mad at me?"

"No, I want to know."

"You'll find out soon enough." Vonte' pulled in Brian's parking lot, got the food out of the truck and the kids ran outside. He kissed his boys and handed Nikki their food. Diamond had to laugh at herself for acting like a baby because Vonte' was playing mind games with her and she was falling for them. They pulled back in their driveway, he got out of his truck, went into the house and closed the door. Diamond sat there for a second and realized that he wasn't coming back. Vonte' had gone into the house, lit the candles that he had on the table and poured some silk rose petals on the floor from the door to the kitchen table. He washed his hands and put on his apron just as Diamond walked through the door.

"You could have said you wasn't coming back." Diamond smelt something sweet and noticed the rose petals, so she took off her shoes and smiled as she followed the trail. She sat at the table and Vonte' began to serve her with ribs that he had spent all day grilling, homemade macaroni and cheese, collard greens, dinner rolls and potato salad. She got up quickly and washed her hands, Vonte' blessed the food and they enjoyed their meal. For dessert Vonte' had made strawberry shortcake with one huge strawberry that had been cut in half and filled with cool whip. He sat next to her and fed her the strawberry with a little cool whip and handed her the other half. Diamond licked the cream and was about to take a bite when she felt something hard. Vonte' started smiling. She looked down and there was a one karat diamond ring that Vonte' had been paying on since he started his job at Motor Company and had used the thousand dollars to get it out of layaway.

"Baby, I'm ready to make this official and I didn't want to do it until I was able to do it right. Will you marry me?"

Diamond started to cry because she never imagined. This was the best birthday that she had ever had. Vonte' put the ring on her finger and he kissed her tears away. He picked her up and carried her upstairs to their bedroom where there were red lights, and the twelfth rose was torn up and the petals were laid across the bed.

"Yes Vonte', I will marry you." Vonte' undressed his wife-to-be and made love to her like it was their first time. Afterwards, they took a nice warm shower. A couple hours later, a few of their friends came by and Brian brought the kids home. They played games and listened to music until the sun came up and of course, Diamond shared the good news with everyone. Brian already knew because Vonte' had asked his permission to marry his daughter and he gave them his blessing.

On Saturday, May twenty sixth at two forty-five in the afternoon, Diamond and Vonte' walked down the aisle of Random Baptist Church. Diamond wore a long, strapless sky-blue dress that showed her figure. It was lacey in the front with silver rhinestones across the chest and her stomach. There was an angel hanging in each corner of the church by the pulpit and it was beautifully decorated in sky blue and maroon. Nikki and Chrissy were her bridesmaids and Vonte' Jr. was the ring bearer. Vonte's best men were Rob, Rick and Johnny, his childhood best friends. Instead of a limo they had a white horse and a carriage, they released two white doves and a couple of pigeons. Erika, Kendra, her husband Greg, Tamika, her man Chris and their kids, Timothy, and Big Tone all put in money on a van. Rosetta and Mario rented a U-Haul and loaded all of Diamond's things from storage and drove to Ohio. Diamond was so happy to see her friends, she didn't even know they were coming, and she hadn't seen them in years.

The next day, Diamond spent with her friends and family. On Wednesday, everyone headed back to Arizona while Vonte' and Diamond left for Florida so they could get on their cruise to the Bahamas.

Diamond and Vonte' are extremely happy. Diamond is supervisor at State Hospital and Vonte' has been working overtime almost every day. They hooked up their house. Diamond took a lot of ideas from Sexxy T's house and applied them to her own. Nikki is glad to be back with her mother and living the life that she always wanted. Vonte' keeps his boys clean and attend Random Baptist Church every Sunday with their three-piece suits and 'gators on. Rosetta and Brian are close friends and are so proud of their daughter. Rosetta gets her grandkids every summer and visits Ohio every Christmas. Brian gets his grandkids every other weekend to give his hard-working daughter a break and to allow some quality time with her husband. Diamond no longer receives social security because Dr. Ford has removed her from her bipolar medicine and so far, she's doing fine.

ABOUT THE AUTHOR

D M Cummings was born and raised in Akron, Ohio. She is a mother of three beautiful little ladies. She attended the University of Akron and has degrees in Computer Programming, Business Management and Medical Office Management

Also By D M Cummings

Is real love worth my life?, which was turned into a stage play that she produced.

Diamond's Pearl
Take a Walk in my Shoes

Coming March 2023
I cried…but I never GAVE UP

www.ingramcontent.com/pod-product-compliance
Lightning Source LLC
Chambersburg PA
CBHW010449100726
47904CB00008B/2539
9780977385416